───────────── ★ ─────────────

My mind kept going back to Caro and the widely differing opinions people had of her. Daniel still thought she was a sweetheart; Mrs. Barcasie said she was a social-climbing tart. I wasn't sure what "tart" encompassed in the Hon. Violet's mind, but it didn't sound good. Sara Lee said she was a no-good tramp; Sarah Leah thought she was a sweet and generous person. Her brother said she was selfish and demanding. My own opinion, based on what I'd heard from others so far, was that she was narcissistic and obsessively self-centered. None of which was fuel for murder.

Somebody obviously had a motive, or thought they did, but it certainly wasn't obvious to me. Caro had more to fear from others than anyone had to fear from her, or so it appeared.

───────────── ★ ─────────────

Previously published Worldwide Mystery titles by
E. L. LARKIN

HEAR MY CRY
HEAR ME DIE

Forthcoming from Worldwide Mystery by
E. L. LARKIN

DEAD MEN DIE

DIE AND DIE

E. L. LARKIN

W★RLDWIDE.

TORONTO • NEW YORK • LONDON
AMSTERDAM • PARIS • SYDNEY • HAMBURG
STOCKHOLM • ATHENS • TOKYO • MILAN
MADRID • WARSAW • BUDAPEST • AUCKLAND

DIE AND DIE

A Worldwide Mystery/November 2001

First published by Thomas Bouregy & Company, Inc.

ISBN 0-373-26403-8

Printed in U.S.A.

With many thanks to my friend and fellow writer, Birdie Etchison.

ONE

HE STOOD IN the shadow of a maple tree, listening, searching the dark for movement, making sure none of the houses along the alley had lighted windows. Even at 3:00 a.m. someone could be awake. Finally, satisfied, he picked up her limp body and walked around the edge of the garage to the side door. He would open the big alley door when he was through, when it didn't matter what anyone saw, when he wanted someone to see her. But for now, until she was dead, he had to be careful. Her breathing, increasingly labored, sounded abnormally loud in the soft silence.

"WAIT A MINUTE," I said, holding my hand in the air like a schoolboy crossing guard. "The neighbor found *what* in your garage?"

"My wife, Caro. She died three years ago,

when we lived in New York, but her body was lying on the floor of my garage.''

As Daniel lived on Forty-seventh and we were sitting in my office on Forty-fifth, in Seattle, Washington, that did not compute, as Martha would say.

"I need help and you're the only private investigator I know I can trust," Daniel said, looking as pitiful as a guy six-foot-four with bright blue eyes and freckles can look.

The lettering on my office door said: DEMARY JONES, RESEARCH AND GENEALOGY, not PRIVATE INVESTIGATOR. C.R.I., Confidential Research and Inquiry, had been a private-eye place when I went to work for George Crane, but it wasn't anymore. I'd inherited the place by default when George died in a senseless drive-by shooting, and I did have a license, but I very rarely took on that kind of work. At least not on purpose.

"I'm not a PI," I said, frowning at him. "I'm a genealogist and researcher, and you know it, Daniel Zimmer, so don't try that one on me."

Daniel sighed and continued to look pitiful. I knew he was putting it on but I couldn't help feeling a bit annoyed that he had come to me for help. Daniel is an INS agent—Immigration and Naturalization Service—and although I don't know that they do many homicide investigations, they certainly do have qualified investigators on their staff who could help Daniel.

"Oh, all right," I said. "Tell me what happened. Start at the beginning."

Daniel took off his glasses and rubbed his eyes. "I suppose the beginning was three years ago when Caro was killed in a plane accident, or I thought she was," he said, putting his glasses back on. "But the important part happened yesterday."

"Hold on," I interrupted. "Let me make sure I have it right. When your wife Caro died, or you thought she did, you were living in New York. Yes?"

He nodded.

"Sometime after that you moved to Seattle and for the last year you have been living in an apartment in the Skyway area until you bought this house and moved out here two weeks ago. Yes?"

He nodded again.

"So why did you move? To the Wallingford district? You never said."

"I wanted a house in a nice, quiet neighborhood."

"Apparently not the best idea you ever had, but go on."

"It sure wasn't. It has been one thing after another," he said, his expression glum. "But that doesn't have anything to do with Caro. Sunday morning one of my neighbors, a cute little old lady named Mrs. Taylor, walked down the alley between our houses on her way to church. The overhead door to my garage was open; she glanced in as she went by and she saw a dead woman lying on the floor behind my car."

"How did she know the woman was dead?"

"It's an old neighborhood, as you know; the alleys are very narrow and the garages are built practically flush with the property line. With the garage door open, Caro was lying in full view. No one could have missed seeing her, nor could Mrs. Taylor not realize she was dead. Her throat was cut from ear to ear."

"Yuck! How horrible. And I suppose there was blood all over."

"No. I was surprised. There was hardly any blood at all."

That didn't seem possible but I didn't comment.

"She went back home and called the police and after a while they came and rang my doorbell and woke me up and took me out there to see if I could identify her."

"How did they know she was your wife?"

"They didn't. They thought she was a Mrs. Gray who lives three houses up the alley, but she was in my garage so they... At first I..." He stopped, looking away as he shifted uncomfortably in his chair. The freckles on his round choirboy face stood out like paint spots. "I thought I was either hallucinating or losing my mind. Caro has been dead three years and there she was, lying in my garage with her throat cut. I think I must have gone into shock; I can't even remember the next hour or so. I guess there was a lot of confusion."

I could believe that.

"Things got more or less sorted out after a while and they took her body away. They asked me a lot of questions, where I'd been the night before, when I got home, all that kind of stuff,

and took it all down. I'd been at a housewarm-
ing party for a couple I know. They wanted me
to sign a statement but—"

"Whoa. What kind of a statement? Did they
Mirandize you?"

He smiled faintly. "No, not that kind of a
statement, Demary. Even in shock I'm not that
stupid. Just the details of her death in the plane
crash but, as I started to say, I told them I
wasn't signing anything until I had a chance to
get my head together, or without another lawyer
present."

"Another lawyer? Who was the first one?"

"Me."

"I didn't know you had a law degree."

He nodded. "I don't use it particularly, but I
have one."

"Well, go on," I said, thinking that despite
knowing Daniel for quite sometime he was still
a relative stranger.

"That's all. They left and that was that."

"What do you mean, that's all? Obviously
you don't know how she came to be in the garage or how it happened that she wasn't on the
plane, but how about the Mrs. Gray business?
Why did Mrs. Taylor think her name was Gray?

And how sure are you that she was Caro? She would be two years older, and dead—particularly in that way—she would look different.''

''It was Caro.'' He shuddered, his face grim. ''Among other things, the outside edge of the little finger on her left hand has a long thin scar she got when we were first married. She sliced it on the lid of a coffee can she was opening.''

''Well, what about the Mrs. Gray part? Did she get a divorce without notifying you?''

He gave me a surprised look. ''Oh, no, Demary. She wasn't that kind of person. She wouldn't have done anything like that.''

''Well, what do you think happened?''

''I...I don't know. Some kind of amnesia is what I think must have happened.''

''When? I mean, you put her on the plane and then...''

''No, I didn't put her on the plane. The plane left at two-fifteen. I was at work. She took a cab to the airport. When the airline notified me that the plane had gone down I checked with the cab company immediately. Hoping, of course, that she'd taken another plane or something. But the driver said he'd let her off at the right departure gate and saw her take her baggage to the curbside check-in. That was all he knew.''

"Hmm. You think something happened to her at the airport?''

"It must have. She couldn't have been on the plane. It went down in the Rocky Mountains west of Denver, and even if she'd survived the crash she couldn't have walked out. No one could have. There was a blizzard going on. They couldn't even get a team in to recover the bodies for two weeks. Some were never recovered.''

I didn't say anything but I had my doubts. True amnesia isn't all that common, plus how had she arrived in Seattle?

"All I know for sure is she has been living in the neighborhood as Mrs. Steven Gray for at least a year,'' Daniel said unhappily. "She and her husband.''

"What did he have to say?''

Daniel shook his head. "I have no idea. He wasn't home yesterday morning and beyond that I haven't a clue.''

"For heaven's sake, what have you been doing? It's Monday morning. In fact it's nearly noon. Have you talked to the detective in charge? What has he got to say?"

"I haven't been able to contact him and no one else will talk to me. I guess that's what I want you to do, Demary. Find out what's going on. I just don't seem to be able to get myself together enough to...Anyway, I will hire a lawyer as soon as I can contact her."

"Who?"

"Anna Carmine. Her office is here in your building."

I nodded. That was smart of him. Anna was a sharp attorney. "Who's the detective in charge of the case?"

"Lieutenant Sam Morgan."

I might have known it.

TWO

DANIEL WENT ON to fill in a few more details about Caro. Her parents were both dead; her only relative as far as he knew was a half-brother, Roger Crawford. He took a picture of her out of his wallet and put it on the desk. She was a superbeauty with deep blue eyes, silver-blond hair, and a knockout smile.

"She's gorgeous," I said, turning it around to catch the light.

Daniel nodded. "She had a sweet personality," he said in a tired voice. "I have to admit she could be as cranky as a two-year-old when she didn't get her own way, but she was such a sweetheart, that didn't happen often. She was an adorable child too, and looking the way she did, everyone spoiled her from the time she was born."

"Let's go back to when she left New York. Where was she going?"

"Actually she was coming here, or rather, to Bellevue. Her half-brother lives there, or did, anyway. I don't know him. I don't think I've spoken to him more than two or three times. Never, since Caro died." He winced. "Since the plane crash."

I picked up a pen and pulled a legal pad out of my drawer. "What's his name again?"

"Roger Crawford. Caro's mother married twice. Roger was by her first husband, Paul Crawford. Caro by her second, Joe Peters."

"Do you have an address for Crawford?"

"Not anymore, but he should be in the phone book. He owned a small business and apartment complex, the Crawford Building, somewhere in the Bellevue area. He lived in one of the units. Probably still does."

I jotted down the names. "Why didn't you have any contact? Were they estranged? And if so, why was she coming out here? Or wasn't she intending to see him?"

He got up and went over to examine the quilted wall hanging I'd recently put up in place of the citrus-colored wool one. "We hadn't been getting along," he said finally, still staring at the flame-colored quilt. "She said she wanted time alone to decide how she felt, and Seattle was just a place to go. Caro married me thinking that the INS was some kind of intelligence outfit. When she discovered I wasn't a second James Bond, she was unhappy." He turned and came back to his chair. "It took me a while to figure that out but I think it was the basic fact. I loved her. To use an old cliché, I was crazy about her, and I think she loved me, but, as I said, I wasn't the larger-than-life figure she'd thought I was, and that wasn't doing our marriage any good."

Which still didn't answer my question about her brother, so I asked again. "So you don't actually know that she was coming to stay with her brother? She may have had other plans?"

He shook his head. "I don't think so," he said finally. "I know she called him the night before she left and told him what plane she'd be on."

"But you didn't talk to him. Why not?"

"To tell the truth, I don't know why not. I don't think he and Caro were actually, as you call it, estranged, Caro just didn't have much contact with him, so I hadn't either. I guess they didn't have much in common. Plus, of course, he had lived out here ever since he went to college and she lived in New York.''

''Didn't he come to your wedding?''

''No.'' He didn't elaborate, and his attitude told me not to push that one.

''How long were you married before she… uh…before the plane crash?''

''Nine months.''

I started to ask him for dates but just then Martha stuck her head in the door and said Anna Carmine had come in and was in her office. She had time to see Daniel if he came over right away. I told him to go and come back when he finished with her. I had another appointment in a half hour and I wanted to call Sam.

Sam and I go back a long way, back to when I first got out of high school and thought flowerpower could change the world. It didn't take me long, however, to realize the age of Aquarius was long past and that real life wasn't anything like what the fantasy brokers claimed. I went back to school, earned my degree in research, and went to work.

I didn't know Sam all that well then. We had, and have, an on-again, off-again relationship that has had some rowdy ups and downs. Sometimes we are so provoked by each other we barely speak, yet at one time we thought about getting married. Fortunately we came to our senses before that idea went too far. Lately we have been getting along quite well again. Actually, very well. I had even cooked him a birthday dinner Saturday night.

He was not particularly pleased to hear from me.

"Why do you always get mixed up in these things, Demary?" he grumbled.

"I'm not mixed up in it," I protested. "Daniel is a friend and I told him I'd find out what I could. That's all. He's understandably upset. As far as he knew his wife had been dead for three years, and to have her body show up in his garage was something of a shock, to say the least."

"Did you ever consider that he may have put her there?"

"He could have," I admitted. "But why should he? He doesn't have any motive."

"You don't call finding your wife living with another man sufficient motive?"

"Not really. It's been a long time since he saw her. He hasn't forgotten her by any means, but...And anyway, you saw him yesterday. You saw how shocked he was. Do you think he's a good enough actor to fake it?"

Sam made a noncommittal noise that meant he agreed with me but wasn't going to say so. "How long have you known him?" he asked.

"About six months. I met him at a genealogy seminar. He's an INS agent."

"No, actually he isn't an agent. I talked to the local director. He's what they call a civilian employee. They wouldn't say what he does."

"Oh." That was surprising, although I didn't know why it should be. Daniel had never had much to say about his job. We weren't close friends.

"What did her husband, or whatever he is, have to say? Steven Gray, I mean." It's hard to tell in advance what Sam will share with me. Sometimes very little, depending on the case and how well we're getting along. This time he didn't hesitate.

"So far, nothing. We haven't located him yet. He's out of town on business. According to his secretary he was supposed to check in to the Mark Hopkins in San Francisco Friday morning, speak at a dinner that night, and return to Seattle the following day. He did speak at the dinner but didn't stay at the hotel and as far as she knows he hasn't returned. We're working on it."

"Where or how did Caro get off her plane?"

"We don't know that either. The plane made two stops, Chicago and Denver, so she could have gotten off at either one. Or she may not have been on the flight to start with."

"Wouldn't the passenger manifest show whether she was on board or not?"

"Should have, but that doesn't mean it did. I don't know, Demary, I don't have that much information yet. I will tell you this much though. It does look as if your friend Daniel is in the clear. The woman died somewhere between twelve and three, give or take an hour on either end, and according to the people he was with Saturday night he didn't leave their house until after three.''

''Who told…uh…when did you get the medical examiner's report?'' I asked, nearly biting my tongue in my effort to change gears in mid-sentence. I was sure Daniel had said he got home before two.

''About an hour ago.''

''Then she must have been killed somewhere else. Right? And put in the garage after he got home. Daniel says there was no blood around and there certainly should have been.''

''Looks that way.''

We talked a few minutes longer, then hung up. Martha had buzzed me that my appointment had arrived.

My appointment was with the Honorable Violet Barcasie. I'd never met her; she'd been referred to me by another client, Robert Stone. I don't know why but when I stood up to greet her I was expecting a highly polished female of indeterminate age. The lady who came in was of indeterminate age all right, but nothing else I'd expected. Somewhere between fifty and seventy, Violet was a tall, horsey woman, with sandy, flyaway hair half tucked under a battered safari hat, sharp gray eyes, and a loud voice.

"Ah-ha, Ms. Jones," she boomed, coming forward with her hand outstretched. "You're just as Robert described you."

She had a grip like a lumberjack's and shook my hand so vigorously she nearly dislocated my shoulder. How the Honorable Violet acquired her title—or if she was even entitled to it—I never inquired. It fit her. Although anyone more unlike my mental vision of a woman named Violet would be hard to find.

She pulled one of the tangerine-colored chairs around and prepared to sit down. "I'm thinking of buying an expensive painting, an old master, and I want you to check the provenance," she went on before I could respond to her greeting. "Robert said you had done the same—"

She stopped abruptly, her gaze fastened on Caro's picture. Daniel had left it on my desk.

"What are you doing with a picture of that woman?" she demanded. "Did you know that someone cut her throat? Outrageous to say so, but I've never known anyone who deserved it more."

THREE

I SWALLOWED A SQUAWK of surprise. "Uh, you knew Mrs....uh...Mrs. Gray?" I asked. A stupid question if I've ever asked one. She had picked up Caro's picture and was looking at it with distinct aversion.

"Certainly. Everyone in the neighborhood knew the woman. In my day she would have been called a tart."

"I didn't know her," I said faintly. "And I live around here."

"No. Your house is on Forty-sixth. The Gray house is on Forty-eighth and Burke. You aren't that close a neighbor and you don't frequent the same milieu."

That left me flatfooted. "What milieu is that?" I asked, wondering if in fact I knew what the word meant.

"Places that appeal to idle women who have nothing better to do than primp and preen," she said, giving me a considered examination. "You're a woman of good sense and decent appearance. You take care of yourself without wasting anytime on the job."

That did not sound like a compliment. I'm a scant five foot two, stay in reasonably good shape via water aerobics, have blue eyes, a rosy complexion, and curly auburn hair that I keep cut short because it will do its own thing regardless of what I try. No cover girl, but "decent appearance" seemed a bit cold. I'd spent at least five minutes on my makeup that morning.

"How well did you know Caro?" I asked. She obviously didn't think her the sweet young thing Daniel described.

"I didn't know her personally at all, but the wretched woman lived across the street from me so I was bound to hear all about her whether I wanted to or not."

"Would you mind telling me what you've heard?"

She frowned. "Tittle-tattle, gossip, that's all I know, and nothing I'd care to repeat."

Violet showed her teeth in a sudden acid smile. "I will tell you this, however. The woman was a delusional social climber. She had no use for anyone in the neighborhood, no one was grand enough, and she certainly had nothing to do with anyone my age. That is, until she discovered I had a title. Then she would have been glad to make my acquaintance. However, that isn't what I'm here for. So, shall we get to my business?''

I agreed hastily. The Honorable Violet had a way of speaking that got her point across; she wasn't there to answer my questions.

She settled herself firmly in her chair before she spoke. "My husband, my first husband, Charles, was a tool-and diemaker, a drop-forge blacksmith. His hobby was the history and study of the old masters and their work. Particularly the old and less well-known European masters. One of those he came to admire was Georges de La Tour.''

"I don't recognize the name. Was he French?''

She nodded. "Yes, from the province of Lorraine. He died in 1652. He was well known in his time but forgotten after his death and only came back into notice recently. Charles saw some of his work when we were in Paris in 1972 and became enamored of it but was unable to purchase anything he'd done.''

"Why not? Had they become prohibitively expensive?'' I knew some old masters sold in the multimillion-dollar range.

"Yes, of course. But that wasn't the main problem. Charles patented a gizmo of some kind back in the late fifties that made a great deal of money. No, the problem was that there were none for sale. Now, however, I believe I have a chance to acquire one and I want you to check it out before I go any further.''

I pulled a legal pad out of my desk drawer and jotted down the name La Tour. "You said 'acquire' rather than purchase. Are there conditions to the sale? And what gallery are you getting it from?''

"I'm buying it from a man named Adam Parrick. And yes, there is a condition, a very minor one and not a problem. According to Mr. Parrick, his grandfather bought the painting in a small gallery in Cologne in late 1936. He intended it for the dining room of his home. The picture is one of several La Tour is reputed to have done that depicts a cardsharp fleecing a smug young innocent. The then Mrs. Parrick was a staunch antigambling advocate and refused to have it hung. It was relegated to the attic where it has remained until the present time.''

''When Mr. Parrick rediscovered it?''

''Rediscovered? No, it wasn't forgotten. The family knew it was there, but no one had ever particularly liked it, nor realized its value until recently when an article in a magazine alerted them to what they had.''

''You say family. How many claim ownership, or part ownership?''

''As an only child—his father died shortly after he was born—Mr. Adam Parrick is sole owner. His father was an only child also. There is no problem there. He does have a number of children and grandchildren, but they don't enter into it.''

''So what is Mr. Parrick's condition of sale?''

''He would like to donate the picture to a museum in his grandfather's name, but considering what the picture is worth they can't afford to do so. The Parricks are not that well off. I too want to donate it to a museum, and

I can afford to do so, but I want it in Charles's name. We are working on a compromise that will include both men's names.''

I made more notes on my pad. Something about her story bothered me but I couldn't catch hold of what it was.

"What, exactly, is it you want me to do, Mrs. Barcasie? You seem satisfied with your arrangement with Mr. Parrick.''

"I want to know if it's a genuine Georges de La Tour, of course, and I'll have it authenticated by an expert, but I also want to be sure I'm not buying a stolen work. The Nazis had already seized many of the Jews' possessions by the late thirties and the gallery is no longer in business, so tracing its provenance may not be easy. But, as you know, art records were and are kept by a number of agencies, including those of the Nazis. That is what I want you to do. Trace its provenance.''

She opened her handbag, a tapestry affair the size of a small suitcase, and extracted a sheaf of papers.

"These are copies of the original receipt, the shipping orders and invoices. They are a bit blurred in spots but still quite readable.

And here are several excellent snapshots of the picture itself. Three are close-ups of individual faces. It's a beautiful painting.''

I snapped on my desk lamp and examined the gallery receipt. Even in the copy it appeared to be in excellent condition, considering that it was over sixty years old. Maybe too good.

"Where have these papers been kept?'' I asked neutrally.

"In a large manila envelope taped to the back of the picture's frame. As you can see in the snapshots it's one of those huge baroque gilt affairs that were so popular then. The snaps are recent, of course.''

I thought for a minute. Violet waited impatiently.

"How did you and Mr. Parrick get together?'' I asked finally.

"Totally by chance,'' she said, beaming at me. "About a month ago now I got into conversation with a young man at the museum who happened to be admiring the same Rembrandt I was looking at. We chatted a bit and he mentioned that his grandfather had a La Tour. It was a real miracle.''

Chance, my foot. I don't believe in miracles either.

FOUR

I DIDN'T TELL Violet I thought she was being scammed. In the first place I didn't think she'd believe me, and I could be wrong too. I'd been wrong a couple of times before. Plus, if I didn't take the job she would simply hire someone else. Besides, it probably wouldn't take me more than a couple of phone calls to check on Adam Parrick. From the sound of the "chance" meeting, he no doubt had a rap sheet a yard long.

The kind of coincidence she described didn't just happen, it was very carefully designed and orchestrated.

After I agreed to work on the provenance of the La Tour—Parrick, actually—I persuaded Violet to tell me a bit more about Caro. I was careful not to ask for any "tittle-tattle." I wanted to know where Caro spent her time if, as Violet said, she didn't work.

It seemed her main occupations were shopping at the big downtown stores such as Nordstrom and The Bon Marché, and getting her hair done at a pricey beauty salon in one of the high-rise buildings that were turning downtown Seattle into a maze of sunless canyons. Although I did have to admit the view from the fiftieth floor of the Columbia Tower was something spectacular. The salon Caro patronized was so exclusive it didn't even have a name. It was simply known by its suite number. The 5001.

Caro also had worked out at a chic health club on East Garfield that overlooked Lake Washington and the Cascade Mountains in the distance.

If Caro had hidden her past as well as she appeared to have done, the reason for her murder had to be here in Seattle. Either in who she knew or what she had done since she came, so the first thing I needed to do was track her around, find out who her friends were, how she had met Gray, when they were married, and anything else that might have a bearing on her death.

"Are you getting paid for this?" Martha demanded when I told her I was going to go take a look at the health club. She thinks I spend too much time working on nonessentials. Her definition of nonessentials being anything that doesn't pay what she deems I'm worth.

Martha runs my life, or tries to. Technically she is my secretary/associate, and the receptionist for the other tenants in the building. Mostly she is whatever she feels like being. Black and beautiful, she is an even six feet tall with a figure like a board and classic Grecian features. Born in Barbados and raised in Liverpool, England, she still speaks with a broad English accent despite the years she has lived in the U.S. She has a caustic tongue and thinks nothing of using it on me, or anyone else for that matter.

"Of course I'm getting paid," I said innocently. I'd forgotten to talk about pay with Daniel. "Didn't Mrs. Barcasie sign the contract?"

"I'm talking about Daniel Zimmer. I know he's a friend but—"

"I hope I'm a friend but I'll still sign a contract as soon as you get one made out," Daniel said, coming back down the hall and into the reception room. He gave her one of his little-boy-lost smiles.

"Good," Martha said, unabashed and unimpressed.

I couldn't help laughing. When it comes to money—which I am quite fond of myself—Martha has all the flexibility of a brick.

"C'mon, Daniel, let's go over and take a look at the…uh…at your house," I said. I'd started to say the "crime scene" but decided that wouldn't be too tactful. Regardless of other things involved, he'd loved Caro once and she'd been his wife.

IT WAS AN OLD 1930s house, typical of the area, that had been well taken care of over the years. Bungalow style, with a beautiful rose brick fireplace, all hardwood floors, and a recently remodeled kitchen, it had a lot of charm all by itself. There were practically no furnishings; a recliner, small table, and T.V. in the front room; nothing in the dining room; the normal appliances and a white plastic patio table with two chairs in the kitchen; a bed, dresser, and one nightstand in the bedroom. The second bedroom held a collection of boxes that looked as if they contained books.

"Well, what do you think?" Daniel asked after he had shown me around.

I wanted to ask why he didn't have any furniture but decided not. "I think you made a good buy," I said instead. "It's a really neat place. What did you mean earlier when you said there had been one thing after another going wrong? The plumbing? Heating? What?"

He frowned, rubbing his forehead. "No, not that kind of thing and not exactly wrong either, or at least not with the house, but ever since I actually moved in one silly thing after another has happened. I came home one evening to find the whole backyard flooded. Someone had turned on both garden water taps full force. The lawn was a regular lake. Another time all the shrubs in the back had been spray-painted bright red."

"That's vandalism! Did you report it?"

"Uh...well...no. I—I figured it was the neighborhood kids and I didn't want to start anything. I'm the new guy on the block, and

I... Well anyway, I didn't, but a couple of days ago things changed. I've been getting nuisance calls at all hours of the night, and Thursday night I got a threat.''

"Daniel, for heaven's sake. You can't ignore something like that. What kind of a threat was it?''

"It was ridiculous is what it was. A muffled voice saying I'd be sorry if I didn't get out of town. Whoever it was sounded like they either had a bad cold or were talking with their mouth full of marbles.''

"Was it a man or a woman? Could you tell? And did they identify you by name?''

"The voice was too muted to tell whether it was male or female or even if it was an adult. And I have done something. I talked to the phone company and they are going to run a cross tap. But they'll probably never call again.''

I scowled. "What's a cross tap? And why are you so sure they won't call? I have a feeling you aren't telling me something, Daniel. What?''

He gave me a somewhat strained smile. "Forget the cross tap, Demary. I shouldn't have said...Uh...it's something my office, uh..."

"It's borderline legal? Is that it?"

"Umm, yes, I guess you might say so."

"All right, I never heard that part. But you haven't answered my question. What makes you so sure he, or she, won't call again?"

He didn't reply at once. "I think maybe they're too smart," he said finally.

"They? Who? What are you leaving out?" I was beginning to get ticked off. I can't, I won't, work with or for anyone who only tells me half the story. And he knew better. Whatever he did for INS, that was a given. Any kind of an investigator has to have the whole picture to do the job.

"Well, what?" I asked again.

He stumbled around talking rubbish but finally came out with it. The house had formerly belonged to a Colombian drug ring. It had been confiscated by the DEA some years ago and only released for sale in the last six months.

"You bought it knowing that?" I asked, flabbergasted. "And you're surprised to be getting funny-bunny calls in the middle of the night? You didn't just fall off the back of a turnip truck, did you, Daniel? I'm surprised they haven't been throwing rocks through the front window."

"Oh come on, Demary. Don't be silly. The place was owned by a cartel that was broken up nearly five years ago. Why should they be bothering with it now?"

"Well, at a guess, because they don't want anyone living here," I said absently, my mind flipping back to the reason I was there to start with.

Caro. How did she fit into the drug picture?

FIVE

WHEN I GOT BACK to the office I called the 5001 where Caro had her hair done but they couldn't give me an appointment for three weeks, and didn't sound as if they wanted to give me one then. I doubted that I'd want one by that time; all I was interested in was hearing the gossip about Caro that was undoubtedly going around right now, but I went ahead and booked a shampoo and cut anyway. I asked for Raphael, the man who did Caro's hair, thinking I might learn something from him even after that long if I went at it right. In the meantime I'd call my high-school buddy, Sherry Hall, and see if she could tell me how to get in right away. I knew she could get her hair done at any shop in town on fifteen minutes' notice.

Of course, she was a top runway model who

worked all the international shows, which possibly made a difference.

I had spent a half hour in Daniel's backyard and in the alley before I came back to the office. I wasn't looking for anything in particular; if there had been anything to find, the crime scene boys would have found it already. I just wanted to get the general layout in my head.

When I walked down to the end and stepped out of the alley to check how much of his yard was visible from the cross street, I was nearly run down by a couple of skateboarders. One of whom was my teenage pal, Joey Winters.

"Watch where you're going, Demary!" he'd screeched, more startled than I. "You're gonna be riding your beam-end if you don't look alive."

It took me a minute to figure that out, and by the time I did he was two blocks away, going at an incredible rate of speed. I'd made a mental note to call him later, so I decided to do it now before I phoned Sherry.

Joey is thirteen, thin, wiry, and small for his age, with sandy blond hair, freckles, and an engaging smile despite a full set of braces.

He's smart-mouthed and speaks a language all his own but he's the kind of kid who not only knows everybody in the neighborhood, he knows everything that's going on in the neighborhood. If he was accustomed to hanging out anywhere near Daniel's house he not only could, but probably did, know all about Caro's death, plus all the neighborhood gossip.

He wasn't home but his mother said she'd have him call me. Mrs. Winters is a pleasant lady with a rather vague manner. I've met her several times and she knows what I do for a living but she didn't seem to think it at all strange that I should be asking for Joey. Joey's father is an airline pilot; he's away from home a lot, and it's obvious that in his absence Joey looks after his mother rather than the other way around. He is very protective of her, very attentive. If he is away from the neighborhood he always calls her at least once, although I sometimes wonder if he doesn't call to make sure she is all right rather than to reassure her that he is.

Sherry was at home and delighted to hear from me. She is one of the nicest people I have ever known, which in my experience is some-

what atypical for a female as lovely in looks
and personality as she has always been.

When we were growing up and all our
friends started developing physically, Sherry
simply got taller and cried a lot. Then her
mother sent her to a charm school and the rest
was inevitable. She went to work for a model
agency when she was still in high school and
eventually became one of the top ten models
in the country. She is five eleven, still has
only minimal curves, wonderful cheekbones,
straight, dark brown hair that hangs to her
shoulders in a natural curve, and photographs
like a dream. The perfect model.

She is a sweetie but, unfortunately, much
too trusting. She not only believes anything
anyone tells her, she's a pushover for any kind
of sob story. A personality flaw I've been trying to correct ever since we were teenagers.
She doesn't seem to grasp the concept of skepticism.

To my surprise she knew all about Caro's
death. She'd had her hair done that morning
in preparation for a job she was leaving for
that afternoon.

"Where did you say?" I asked, thinking I'd misunderstood.

"Iceland. Isn't that the limit on about three hours' notice? But on the other hand I'm glad they aren't going to set up in the Westlake Mall, which was the original idea. It's a photo shoot for a spread in *Elle* and I'll be wearing the newest in ski apparel, boots, ski poles, the whole nine yards."

I could see her point. It was close to ninety out. Very unusual for September in Seattle. El Nino had a lot to be blamed for. Certainly not the day to be modeling ski wear on the street.

"What did Raphael have to say about Caro?" I asked, thinking again what a silly name that was for a man.

"He rather liked her, or at least that was what he said, but I didn't much believe him. No one else in the place had a good word to say about her and I think he was just trying to show the other women getting their hair done that he didn't tell tales out of school. Mari, the shampoo girl, said Caro was a pain in the neck. Always claiming Mari got water in her ears, or down her neck, or on her arm. Just anything she could whine about to Raphael and get him to sweet-talk her.''

"Do you think they had something going?"

"Heavens no. I've known Ralph for years. He's one-hundred-and-ten-percent business. He'd never jeopardize his position that way."

"Ralph?"

"Oh, dear. Forget I said that, please. It slipped out. His name is actually Ralph Schultz but he knew that would never do for a top-of-the-line stylist, so he changed it as soon as he got a job. He lived next door to my cousin when we were kids."

"I'll never tell," I said, grinning at my reflection in the computer screen. "Did you hear any other comments about Caro?"

"Nothing specific, but no one had anything good to say about her either. And one of the women there, her name is Ruth something, knew Steven's first wife, Nancy, who, according to her, is a really nice person. And, again according to her, Caro was the one who lured Steven, not the other way around."

"Bull cookies. If he was any kind of man he couldn't be lured."

"Hmm. I don't know. A woman as gorgeous as Caro could tempt a saint. Even my photographer, Scott, thinks she's stunning, and he sees nothing but beautiful women everyday."

"You sound as if you knew her."

"Not really. Know her, I mean, but I have seen her any number of times. We go to the same beauty shop, of course, and also to the same health club. Cascade View. If you want some opinions on Caro that's where you ought to go."

"Why?"

Sherry giggled. "'Cause she was one of those women who has a perfect figure and didn't have to do a darn thing to maintain it. That can generate a lot of dislike among the rest of us who have to work like maniacs just to stay in reasonable shape."

Reasonable shape? Wow. I'd like to have what Sherry considered reasonable shape.

"What did she do at the health club then?"

"Mostly spent her time lying around the pool showing off said figure in a bikini. But I do have to admit both she and her cronies watched what they ate. In fact I think Caro existed on celery sticks and carrots. She didn't drink either, so that helped.''

"Do you know the names of any of her friends? I think I'll go out there and see what I can hear.''

"You have to belong to get in but I'll call and get you a guest card. And no, I don't know any of her friends except Sara Lee, but talk to her first and she'll introduce you around. Don't tell her you're a PI, though. She's paranoid her husband will find out and dump her.''

"Oh?'' My snoop factor went into high gear. "Find out what?''

Sherry whooped with laughter. "Find out she isn't the femme fatale she has him convinced she is. He's afraid she's got a boyfriend and of course she hasn't got anything of the kind. He's been trying for months to catch her and one of these days he's going to find out she just goes to the gym everyday.''

SIX

MARTHA STUCK HER HEAD in the door just as I hung up. "You may have figured Parrick wrong," she said, frowning. "Are you sure you have his name correct?"

"Yes. Mrs. Barcasie spelled it for me. Why? Can't you trace him?" I'd told her to do a background check on him before I left with Daniel to see his house.

"I found him all right, but he looks as pure as spring water. No criminal record of any kind. Not even a speeding ticket. His credit record is A-1, he owns his house free and clear, and has had the same wife for forty-two years."

I didn't ask her if she was sure. Martha is as good as I am at that kind of thing. But I still thought the Hon. Violet had been set up. This just meant the scam was a little more so-phisticated than I'd expected.

"What kind of work does he do?"

"He's a printer/engraver for the Ardis Company. Very upscale old company. They do wedding invitations, graduation announcements, that kind of thing. He's been with them twenty-two years."

"Hmm. I think Sherry has done some work for them. Posed for some kind of a letterhead. I wonder if she knows him." I reached for the phone then pulled my hand back. She would be rushing around getting ready to go. I'd call when she got back. It wasn't all that pressing. First I'd go see him, a perfectly normal thing to do if Mrs. Barcasie had told him I would be authenticating the work as she'd said she'd do.

The phone rang in the other room and Martha went back out to answer it. I shelved the La Tour problem for the moment and got busy on my computer, opening a file on Carolyn (Caro) Peters/Zimmer/Gray. I wasn't sure the Gray was legal, but it didn't really matter if it was or not. People here knew her as Caro Gray. I keyboarded in everything I knew, or had heard, and a few things that were pure guesswork. I think better looking at a computer screen. I closed down a little later when my stomach started making threatening noises. It was after three o'clock.

Martha was still beavering away at her PC and barely nodded when I told her I was on my way down to Dick's Drive-In for a hamburger and fries and asked if she wanted one too.

Joey was doing gymnastics around the NO PARKING sign in front of the office, his skateboard leaning against the door of the new Lexus behind him. I hoped it wouldn't scratch. The car belonged to my uptight office neighbor, Harry Madison. I'd been worried about him lately. The slightest thing, such as someone taking his parking space in back, was apt to send his blood pressure soaring, and someone must have taken it today or he wouldn't be parked out front. A scratch on his new toy would give him apoplexy for sure.

"My mom told me you called. Thought I'd come along and see what you were into," Joey said with his engaging grin. His braces glittered like the crown jewels. I think he polishes them.

Involving Joey in any case I worked on

bothered me sometimes; after all, he was just a kid. But on the other hand he was such a natural-born snoop I couldn't have stopped him if I'd tried. He had elected himself my alter ego sometime ago and nothing I said deterred him.

"You sleuthing the killing over on Forty-eighth? The dame with her throat cut?" he asked. "Not a nice one, that. Nearly scared old Mrs. Taylor into spasms. He shouldn't have done that. She don't need that kind of aggro. The perp should have kept the door down."

A typical Joey viewpoint.

"No, not exactly anyway," I said, answering his question. "Her former husband is a friend of mine, so I'm just trying to keep track of the case for him."

"He the big blond guy that just moved into that old crack house?"

"Crack house? They brewed crack there?"

"Naw, just used the place for a warehouse. Cops cleaned it out a long time ago. I never knew much about it. I'm not into that stuff. Fries your brain."

"I'm glad to hear that. But have you heard

anything else about the house? Since Daniel
moved in, I mean.''

He hesitated slightly, unusual for him.
''Maybe. I'll think about it,'' he said. ''I'll
catch you later.'' Snatching his skateboard off
the car, he zipped away before I could question him any further, leaving me wondering
what he was so reluctant to talk about.

THE CASCADE VIEW Health Club was a surprise. Entering the reception area it looked
pretty standard, clean, practical, very busi-
nesslike, and through the glass wall beyond
the sign-in desk, I could see all the regular
equipment standing in rows. Some in use,
some not. It was a women-only club and from
the Hon. Violet's comments, I had expected
something a bit more lavish, more feminine
and frilly.

After the prelims were taken care of, name,
address, occupation—I wrote *Genealogist* in
that space, which happens to be the truth—I
was taken on a tour of the facility.

Behind the workout area was a short hall
with two handball courts visible through heavy
glass windows. One on each side of the hall.

Still nothing too unusual. Beyond them we went through a set of swinging doors, another short hall, into the pool area, and into another world.

Talk about opulence! The place outdid anything I'd ever even seen pictures of, let alone ever set foot in. The room was huge with a domed glass roof and an oversized free-form pool complete with a Jacuzzi at the near end. The flooring was cedar plank and ankle-deep plush carpeting where there wasn't tile. White wicker chairs and lounges covered with bright cushions, small tables, and colorful lounging mats were grouped around the pool and in small alcoves further back amidst the greenery. A good-sized hot tub set in a grove of pines at the far side was surrounded by a faintly Japanese-looking pavilion built of some very dark, shiny wood with orchid plants trailing down all the support poles. The pines were planted in huge porcelain tubs ornamented with pale, multicolored flowers. The banks of flowers, mostly orchids, and the clumps of exotic ferns around the walls gave the place the look of a tropical rain forest. Against the wall to my left, clusters of palm trees in big

wooden planters overlooked a small bar roofed
with palm thatch and dripping with scarlet
bougainvillea. A young woman dressed—if
you could call it that—in a golden tan and a
couple of strategically placed ribbons was de-
livering a tray of drinks to a table of three
women not far from the entrance.

I had asked for Sara Lee when I came in
and my guide now pointed her out. She was
sitting at a nearby table with a tall frothy drink
in front of her.

"Hi. Are you Demary?" Sara Lee called
out when she saw us. "Connie said you'd be
looking for me this afternoon."

"That's me," I agreed, glad I'd gone home
after my hamburger and changed to a blue-
and-white checked cotton pajama suit that
looked okay in these surroundings. Sara Lee
was wearing a similar outfit in turquoise that
matched her eyes. (I suspected contact lenses
and was catty enough to wonder if she had a
pair to match every costume.)

"Have one of these?" she asked, holding
up her glass. "Wonderful stuff and hardly a
calorie in a carload."

"It looks good. What's in it?" I asked,

thinking I could claim an allergy if it turned
out to be raw beets and unsprouted soybeans.

"Cranberry-raspberry juice, orange sherbet,
and sparkling water."

"Mmm, sounds good. I'll have one."

She signaled the waitress and then turned to
me with a big smile. "Connie said you were
a genealogist and I might be able to help you.
Who are you trying to document?"

Telling the truth—or part of the truth anyway—seemed like a good idea as long as
Sherry had already set it up. "The Dorian
Quesada family. One of our new council-
men," I told her cheerfully. That happened to
be the truth too, and the best part of it was
one of Dorian's antecedents was actually
named Joe Peters. Not Caro's father, but what
the hey, it should work as an opening. And it
did, in spades.

The minute I mentioned the possibility of
Caro Gray being a connection of the council-
man, Sara Lee was off and away. Her opening
remark, delivered in a shrill voice, set the tone.

"You're either mentally deranged or the
worst genealogist on record," she said, slamming her drink down on the table so hard it
was a wonder the glass didn't shatter. "You
can't possibly be a friend of Sherry Hall's!"

SEVEN

THE NEXT COUPLE of minutes were not pleasant. I had pushed the wrong button for sure.

"How dare you say something like that!" she yelled. "Caro Gray was a no-good tramp and saying she was related to the Quesadas is absolute libel."

"Hey!" I yelled right back. "I didn't say anything of the kind. I said they both had a Joe Peters in the family."

She glared at me, breathing heavily.

"Don't be ridiculous," I said in a quieter voice. The jets in the Jacuzzi drowned out most of our conversation—if it could be called that—but we were still attracting considerable attention. "The Quesadas are both Mexican-American. Caro's family comes from New England; it's highly unlikely they would be related to the Quesadas. What's your problem anyway? Are the Quesadas friends of yours?"

To my horror she let out a regular shriek
and burst into tears. At that, a woman in a
brief red swimsuit sitting at another table came
over.

"Sara, are you all right?" she asked, giving
me a sharp look. "Do you want me to call
security? Is this woman bothering—"

"No, no. I'm fine. I'm just making a fool
of myself again is all," Sara Lee wailed, interrupting her. "She said something about
Caro Gray and I...I... Oh, you know." She
put her hands over her face and continued to
cry.

"Oh. All right then." The woman turned
and went back to her table.

For a moment I was tempted to do the same,
get up and leave. It did look as if I'd struck
some kind of a mother lode, however, so it
behooved me to hang in there. I made soothing
noises and within a couple of minutes Sara
Lee used one hand to dig in the big flowered
bag she had hanging on the back of her chair
and got out a handful of tissues.

She mopped her face, shoved her hair back,
and gave me a watery smile. "I'm sorry. That
was stupid of me but I can't seem to help my-

self. Every time I hear her name I have hysterics. It's totally stupid, and I know it."

"I...uh...I'm sorry too. I wouldn't have mentioned her if I'd known you were such dear friends."

"Dear friends?" Her voice rose several octaves before she could get it under control. "Friends? No way was she a friend. I detested her. Really hated her. It was her fault my sister committed suicide."

"Ouch. Look, let's just forget her. I can see you—"

"No, let me tell you," she interrupted. "It might hurt your feelings but you ought to know what kind of a person she really was. She wasn't the sweet, innocent, little thing she pretended to be."

I started to tell her that whatever she said, it wouldn't hurt my feelings, but decided to keep my mouth shut and let her talk.

"My sister, Kathy, is—was—ten years younger than me. She married Don Ward the summer she graduated from high school. They were too young and she was spoiled because she was the baby of the family, so they had some problems but they were working them out and were doing okay until Caro came along."

"How did they meet? Caro and Don?"

"They lived in the same apartment complex. This was before she married Steven. She said she had just moved to Seattle, but that was another of her lies. I found out later she'd been living here for several months. She latched on to Don the day she moved into the apartment by getting a chair stuck in the entryway just as he came home from work. Of course he had to help her."

Sara Lee's bitter voice left no doubt that Caro had gotten stuck deliberately.

"Don went crazy over her. He not only left Kathy, he ended up losing his job, and simply devastating his own family too. His father is a prominent surgeon, Dr. Hubert Ward, and when Don ended up working in a used car lot they were sick. They had spent a fortune on his education, Don had just passed his exams and got his CPA license, and he was almost ready to open his own office. He threw his whole career away for that—that— And then the minute she met Steven, she dumped him."

Sara Lee went on to tell me the rest, in detail, of what was a trite and predictable story. The part that didn't ring true was her sister's suicide. Women didn't commit suicide over unfaithful husbands, not in this day and age. Half the population would be obliterated if they did.

At least not unless they were mentally unstable, but that wasn't a question I could ask. The fact remained: Caro had broken up the marriage.

"I'm sorry," I said inadequately. "It must have been awful for your whole family."

She nodded. "Yes, it was, and is, but you can see why I told you, can't you? And Don never has gotten over her. He still thinks she's a…a—" Her voice was rising again.

"Sara Lee, I think I've given you the wrong impression." I interrupted quickly. "I never knew Caro at all. I never heard of her until this morning. I know her first husband and he—" I remembered just in time not to tell her I was a PI,

"First husband? She was married before? Steven certainly never knew that! And neither did Don." She began to laugh, hysteria close to the surface again. "She was married in our church. Steven's church too. The pastor is very old-fashioned and he always makes out an old-fashioned marriage certificate, fills it in by hand in beautiful copperplate. I saw it, it said Carolyn Annette Peters, spinster! She lied about that too!"

I was about to make an abrupt departure; I didn't want to go through another bout of her weeping and wailing, when she did a sudden three hundred and sixty. Her face stiffened into an angry mask.

"I know you now," she said, her voice icy. "I just realized. I ought to have remembered your name but it never occurred to me that Sherry would do me such a rotten trick. You're Sherry's private snoop. A lousy private investigator."

"I am not a PI," I snapped, my voice as cold as hers. "I'm exactly what Sherry said I was. A certified genealogist. And yes, I do have a PI license, but I don't do that kind of work, at least not normally. In this case, as I said, I'm a friend of her first husband, and yes, I am looking into her death, but purely for his sake, his peace of mind. He needs to know what happened."

"Then what the heck did you want to talk to me about?" she demanded, her eyes still snapping with anger.

"I simply wanted to know more about Caro, and if Sherry is your friend, you know what she's like. Do you think she'd do you dirty in some way?" I said, trying to sound conciliatory as I swallowed my own temper. Sherry certainly hadn't done me a good turn with this introduction. On the other hand, she was notoriously absentminded. She could have forgotten about Sara Lee's sister, or had never heard about her.

After a minute Sara Lee made a shamefaced grimace. "No. She wouldn't. I'm sorry. It's just that everytime I hear Caro's name...When I heard she'd been murdered I cheered."

"Where did you hear?"

She shrugged. "I don't know. It was all over the club when I came in. Someone told me."

I found that a bit hard to believe. The police hadn't made any kind of a statement as yet and neither Caro nor her murder were big enough news to be on the radio or television. One little murder more or less didn't attract

much attention nowadays, not with teenagers
shooting their teachers over bad grades, or
mad bombers blowing up whole buildings. I
was mulling that over in my mind when a tiny
little blond woman dressed in an elegant white
linen dress and high-heeled white sandals
came up to our table.

"Hi, Sara Lee," she chirped.

Sara Lee looked up with a weak smile. "Hi,
yourself, Sara Lee."

"You must be Demary," this second Sara
said to me. "Sherry told me you wanted to
talk to me. Sorry I'm so late."

"You're both Sara Lee? Two of you?" I
asked, feeling stupid.

They both giggled.

I stared at them blankly. Then, belatedly,
my needle-sharp investigator's brain finally
kicked into gear. When I'd come up to the
table, Sara Lee said "Connie" had told her I
was coming. Connie, who must have been the
receptionist, had her Saras confused and I
hadn't picked up on it. The first Sara Lee was
definitely no friend of Caro, as Sherry had
claimed her to be.

In fact, by the sound of it, she could well be Caro's killer. She had motive, or thought she had anyway. As did her ex-brother-in-law, from the sound of things.

EIGHT

THIS SECOND Sara Lee set a different tone with her first sentence.

"It's nearly six o'clock. Let's go somewhere and eat," she said, smiling up at me. An unusual occurrence in my life. At five two I'm usually the one looking up. She was so tiny, even in her high heels, she was like an animated doll. She wasn't the least bit pretty, in fact she was somewhat homely, with eyes too big for her face and a little pug nose. I could see why Sherry was so amused at the woman keeping her husband convinced she was a femme fatale.

She was a forceful little thing, though, and had me saying good-bye to the first Sara Lee and on my way out of the place before I had time to say yea or nay. Very smoothly too.

"I know you must be hungry after listening

to Sara run Caro down for an hour. We can talk over dinner.''

''Uh, she was a bit...'' I hesitated. ''Well, I guess intense would be the word. And yes, I'd love to go eat. Where did you have in mind?''

''There is a great Indonesian place just a block up the street. We can walk. Okay?''

''Sounds good to me.''

We didn't discuss Caro on the way. Instead she talked about herself and the other Sara, telling me her own name was actually Sarah Leah Irvine. The first Sara Lee was just that. Lee was her married name. She seemed reluctant to talk about Caro and I didn't press her. I didn't want her dissolving into tears too. Especially not here on the street. The regulars call this particular area the ''Foot of Madison.'' Madison ends here at Lake Washington, our twenty-five-plus miles of water on the east side of Seattle proper. It's a very mixed district, with pricey high-rise condos, run-down tenements, upscale businesses like Cascade View, and tiny little ethnic groceries, all rubbing along together.

The restaurant, the Komodo Dragon (why

would anyone name a food establishment after a lizard?), had a narrow front entrance that opened into a long hall. At the far end a smiling Indonesian girl ushered us into a surprisingly large dining room with padded booths along two sides, tables in the center, and a great profusion of tropical-looking trees dripping with orchids. I wondered if the local florist had been offering bargain basement prices on the things until I realized these were fake. Actually, very good fakes made of silk.

Sarah, as she told me she preferred to be called, ordered for both of us. The menu selections were all strange to me. So was the food when it arrived. The only thing I recognized was rice. It was all delicious, however.

"Did you know Caro very well, or I guess I should say, very long?" Sarah asked finally.

"No. I didn't know her at all. I'd never heard of her before this morning. I'm simply inquiring into her death for her first husband. He's a friend of mine and, to the police at least, he's a potential suspect."

"First husband?" She looked puzzled rather than shocked. "Are you sure we're talking about the same woman?"

I decided this wasn't going to work. "Yes. I have the right woman. Sherry must have told you I'm a genealogist, which I am, but I also have a private detective's license and a few police contacts. So Daniel, that's her first husband, asked me to look into things for him."

"Sherry didn't mention your being a detective," she said stiffly.

"Probably didn't think it was important," I said neutrally. "That's not the kind of work I do. At least not very often. And I can't say as I'm doing much detecting now either. As I said, Daniel is a friend, so I told him I'd help if I could. He's extremely upset."

"Why are you asking questions about Caro? She's the one who was killed. You can hardly suspect her of anything."

"Of course not. But unless a homicidal maniac just happened to meet her in the alleyway at three o'clock in the morning, the chances are she was killed by someone she knew, and until I know something about her and her friends I'm not going to get very far finding out who that someone was."

She looked down at her plate, picking at the food. "I suppose Sara made it sound as if everyone she knew would have liked to murder her, but that isn't true." She raised her head to stare me in the eye. "Caro couldn't help how she looked, and why should she anyway? She was beautiful and men were attracted to her, but that doesn't mean she was the kind of person Sara claims. She didn't lure Don away from Kathy. They were already having problems. In fact, Caro told me it was several weeks before she even knew Don was married. And he was the one who pursued her, not the other way around. Even after she married Steven."

I found it hard to believe Caro hadn't known he was married if they lived in the same building. But, depending on how interested Caro might have been, it could just possibly be true. So far no one who knew her had claimed she was particularly observant, or even very bright.

"Do you have any ideas?" I asked.

"Ideas? What kind of ideas? About what?"

"About who could have killed her," I said, wondering if she was stonewalling, or just a bit dense. What did she think we were talking about?

"No. And even though you were being sarcastic, I think that's what must have happened. Some total stranger, one of those serial murderers, killed her. No one who knew her would do such a thing."

She actually sounded sincere. She must not have known much about Caro's immediate past to feel that way. "If that was the case you have to wonder what she was doing in the alley in the middle of the night, don't you?" I said, making an effort to keep my tone light.

"She wasn't killed in the alley. There wasn't any blood anywhere around her. She was killed somewhere else and put in that garage there."

She could be right of course, but how did she know so much about it? I knew darn well that part of the scene hadn't been on any news.

"And anyway," she went on, "what makes you think her first husband didn't do it? After all, she was found in his garage. Just because he's your friend doesn't prove his innocence."

"No, it doesn't," I agreed. "But he thought she was already dead."

"What? How could he...I mean, why would he think she was dead?"

I explained about the plane wreck, finishing with his arriving at my office this morning. She didn't say anything for a minute.

"I don't know," she said finally. "The whole thing sounds like some kind of stupid TV thriller. Could he be mistaken? Could Caro simply look like his wife?"

"With the same name? The same maiden name? Carolyn Annette Peters. And anyway, the police will verify her identity. Her prints are on file because of Daniel's job."

"Caro wasn't the kind of person I can see you think she was," Sarah said firmly. "I don't know what happened, either with the plane wreck or her murder, but I do know she was a sweet and generous person. She didn't drink, or smoke, or hang around bars, or run around on Steven, or…or…any of that kind of thing. She wasn't terribly smart and she could have done something she shouldn't and then not known how to get herself out of it, but she wasn't a bad person in any way."

I started to ask her exactly what she meant, but before I could get the words out she stood up and tossed a twenty-dollar bill on the table.

"I'm sorry, Demary, I just don't want to

talk about it anymore. Maybe in a couple of days.''

With that, she turned and walked out. Some leads just don't pan out at all.

NINE

I SPENT THE DRIVE HOME telling myself that maybe I needed to take lessons in how to be more tactful. Talk about a wasted afternoon! This one ranked right up there with thumb twiddling. As far as I could tell all I'd done was to get two people annoyed with me and probably with Sherry as well. I certainly hadn't learned much. Or what I had learned canceled itself out. Sara Lee thought Caro was a rotten person. Sarah Leah thought she was a darling. Neither one of them had really told me much.

By the time I got home I was beating myself bloody for being so incompetent. I hate it when I give myself a pity party like that. So I hadn't achieved anything. So what? I never said I was a female Sherlock Holmes.

I screeched into my driveway and went slamming into the house. Still feeling so down,

I was actually surprised when I saw I had three messages on my answering machine.

One was from Joey. I called him first. The other two were from Sam and I didn't want to talk to him in my present mood. He'd be sure to pick up on it and give me a lecture on minding my own business, which, according to him, should be genealogy and nothing else.

Joey was his usual ebullient self. Whatever had been bothering him earlier was gone.

"Got something you might want to know," he told me. "It's still early. You want to meet me over on Meridian where I was skateboarding this morning?"

"Can't you tell me on the phone?"

"Nope. I'll see you in a few minutes." The phone clicked in my ear.

Muttering to myself, I got back in the car and drove the few blocks to where he had nearly knocked me off my feet earlier in the day. He showed up a few minutes later with two other boys. One his age and one several years younger. I got out of the car to meet them.

"This is Pete Blainey, he's seven," Joey

said, indicating the younger boy. "Bert's his brother."

Bert, the older boy, nodded at me, but didn't speak. He was dressed in what I had to assume was the height of male teenage fashion, as nearly every boy I saw looked the same. Over-sized pants hanging on his hipbones and dragging the ground, topped by a T-shirt that could have housed three his size.

Joey, of course, remained his own man. His jeans and T-shirt fit him reasonably well although both were worn and faded. It was probably a good thing the T-shirt had faded, as what I could see of the writing on the front of it was somewhat risqué, involving a large alley cat in a top hat and carrying a cane.

"He's got something to tell you." Joey gave Pete a slight push in my direction. "Go on, tell her, Pete."

Pete looked at his brother, undecided.

"Tell her," Joey said again. "You're a witness. Tell her what you saw."

"We didn't do it," Pete blurted. "We saw the lady come out and we went and looked but we didn't even go in. It weren't our fault."

Joey sighed theatrically. "That ain't the

way you do it,'' he told Pete. ''Witnesses have to start at the beginning. Start with you and Marty skateboarding down the alley.''

''Oh.'' Pete gave first his brother and then me a questioning look. I nodded, as did his brother. He started again. ''Well, me and Marty was skateboarding, see, up and down the alley, 'cause my mom won't let me go out on the street, see?''

I nodded some more.

''We was coming down to this end, see, and we saw the lady walking around in the crack house yard. We knew it weren't her house but didn't think nothing about it until we was starting back and we saw her when she come out.''

That gave me a jolt. I didn't know kids his age had ever heard of crack.

''She was acting funny is how come we watched her. She come sneaking around the back of the garage lookin' back and forth like she didn't want no one to see her, like someone was after her or somthin','' Pete went on. ''She didn't pay no attention to us though so when she went on up to her own house we went lookin' to see what she were doing, see?'' He gave his brother an anxious glance, then back to me to be sure I was still listening.

I started to ask which house she belonged in but Joey shook his head at me. Pete didn't notice. Now that he was into the story he went plowing right along.

''She'd turned the water on an' left it. You know, where you hook up the hose. There's two of them on that house, see, an' the water was going all over.'' He frowned at me, very serious. ''We was afraid sombody'd blame us, think we was the ones who turned it on, so we got out of there fast. We ain't been back neither. We been boarding in my alley which ain't as good, not so smooth, but we didn't want no one to think it was us.''

Joey patted Pete's shoulder approvingly. ''You make a good witness and nobody's gonna think it was you,'' he said. ''Not now that you told Demary, anyway.''

Pete looked at me.

''Uh, yes. Joey's right. No one will think you did it.''

''Can I go then?''

''Sure, go on,'' Joey told him after giving me a quick glance. He gave the smaller boy

another little pat. Brother Bert said nothing
from start to finish. His role was apparently
chaperon only. The two of them went off
down the alley at a fast clip.

I turned to Joey. "The woman was Caro
Gray?"

"Yep."

"How did you hear about it?"

"All the kids knew. Everybody thought it
was funny. Except Pete and Marty. They were
worried about getting blamed. But Mr. Zimmer never said anything to anybody." Joey
gave me a strange look. "Why didn't he? You
know?"

"Because he did think it was one of the
neighborhood kids and he didn't want to start
out by causing trouble."

Joey thought about that for a minute.
"Smart," he said finally. "She wasn't. She
should have paid attention to the kids. They
was bound to talk, her acting so sneaky. She
must have been one of those people who treat
little kids like they're not there."

Caro was the obvious choice for the vandalism, once you gave it any thought. Certainly not Colombian drug dealers. They might

blow up the place but turning on garden taps wasn't their style. The same with the telephone calls. Caro must have been in an absolute panic when she realized Daniel had moved in practically next door. She wouldn't necessarily have realized that he'd purchased the property, however, and probably hoped she'd make him uncomfortable enough to leave. Not a particularly good plan, but then nothing I'd heard yet indicated that she had good sense.

I got back home a few minutes before nine, unlocking the door just as the phone started to ring. I figured it was Sam again and was going to let the answering machine pick up but decided to surprise him and answer.

I was the one who got the surprise.

My caller introduced himself as Roger Crawford, Caro's brother.

"I hope I'm not calling too late," he said pleasantly. "I just left Daniel's and as he told me you lived in the neighborhood I wondered if we could talk for a few minutes. Could you meet me at the Café Koffee?"

The CK was only a couple of blocks away

on Forty-fifth, so I said sure. Actually I would have agreed if it had been on the other side of town. I'd been trying to think of a way to meet him.

TEN

ROGER CRAWFORD was waiting for me at a corner table. He stood up as I came in and started toward me but I wouldn't have had any trouble recognizing him. He was the male version of Caro with the same silver-blond hair, sky-blue eyes, and knock-'em-dead smile. He was purely gorgeous, in a very masculine way.

"Demary?" He held out his hand.

"Right." I gave him a quick hard shake. I was prepared to dislike him immediately. Guys that good-looking are far too sure of themselves. Always expecting, and usually rightly, an instant conquest.

As it happened the high-wattage smile covered a very low-wattage personality. It seemed to be my day for getting things wrong.

"Daniel described you," he said diffidently. "He said he'd call to let you know I was a reasonably okay guy to have coffee with."

"I can usually judge for myself," I said, more tartly than I intended.

"Uh, sorry, I didn't mean to sound—"

"I'm sorry, I didn't meant it like—"

We both spoke at the same time, stopped in mid-sentence, and then smiled at each other, on my part at least, feeling foolish.

"Shall we start over?" I asked. "I'm very sorry about your sister. It must have been a horrible shock."

"Thank you, and yes it was, but not as bad as it would have been if we'd been close. We haven't been for years."

"Did the police contact you?"

"Yes, a Lieutenant Morgan. He called and then came over to talk to me. I had just come home. I took a few days off last week. I needed some downtime."

I grimaced. "Not a very nice homecoming."

The waitress deposited two mugs of coffee on the table and was rewarded with his devastating smile. She went off looking dazzled.

He shook his head. "No, but as I said, I hadn't even heard from Caro in over a year, so it wasn't as bad as it could have been."

"You knew she was here in Seattle, though? You knew she hadn't been killed in the plane wreck?"

He nodded, his expression set and uncomfortable. "Yes, I knew she was all right, and I knew she had been in Seattle but not for sure that she still was. The last I heard from her she was living in a condo and called to tell me she was going to marry Steven." He stopped, frowning, and thought a minute. "No, I did hear from her after that. The Christmas after she and Steven were married she called to wish me Merry Christmas and invite me to the New Year's party they were giving."

"Did you go?"

"No." He fiddled with his coffee cup, moved the sugar container around, stared at the table, and finally went on. "No, to tell the truth, I didn't want to meet Steven. I never really knew Daniel but I felt so rotten about what she'd done, that terrible airplane stunt, I didn't want to meet this guy and maybe go through the same thing all over again."

"You mean you knew from the beginning that she hadn't been on the plane? Did you tell Lieutenant Morgan that?"

"Yes, of course I did." He moved restlessly. "You'd have to have known Caro to understand. She was selfish and demanding but she could also be such a sweetheart it was hard to resist her. When she called me after the plane crash and asked me not to tell Daniel, I thought she meant just for the moment. I was furious with her, I knew how he must be suffering, but she spun me such a good line I finally agreed."

"Wait a minute," I interrupted. "I don't quite understand. You mean you knew all along that she hadn't been on the plane? She called and told you, and it was supposed to be some kind of a joke?" My voice rose on the last couple of words. I couldn't imagine any kind of a "sweetheart," as he called her, being that cruel, that rotten.

"Good heavens, no. There wouldn't have been anything funny about..." He appeared unnerved by the idea. "No. No, she called me from the airport before the plane ever left to tell me not to meet it as she wasn't coming. She was going out to Fire Island to spend a couple of days with some friends and would call Daniel from there to tell him she hadn't come out here. And as far as I knew at the time, she did call him. Then, minutes after the news of the crash was on the TV, she phoned again and asked me not to contact Daniel, to give her a little time. I thought she meant she was going home to tell him in person but that she didn't want him to know where she'd been. Actually, I figured she'd had too much to drink and wanted to sober up a bit before she faced him.''

I tried not to look as disgusted with the both of them as I felt. "Did she drink a lot?" I asked.

"No, not really, but she loved gin and drank it straight over ice, like the Russians drink vodka, so sometimes she did get pretty sloppy."

"So what did you do when she was listed among the dead?" If he was telling the truth, and despite his apologetic attitude, he hadn't behaved a bit better than his sister. Plus he was telling a different story in regard to her drinking habits.

"I didn't think anything about it at all. I knew she wasn't dead so I simply thought the papers had it wrong."

"And when Daniel called you to tell you about the funeral service?"

He raised his eyebrows in surprise. "He didn't. Why should he? She wasn't dead. I knew she was all right. I never heard from either of them again until she called to tell me she was in Seattle. Which, as I said, wasn't particularly unusual. I had no idea what she'd actually done."

I was sure Daniel had told me he talked to him about the funeral, or memorial service, but possibly not. "And you never called him?"

"No. As I said before, Caro and I were never close after I left home and when I didn't hear from her again I naturally thought everything was fine. In fact, I'd been surprised when she called originally to tell me she was coming to visit. At that time I hadn't heard from her in six or eight months. She'd told me they hadn't been getting along all that well, and frankly I didn't want to get involved in their problems. It simply never occurred to me that she'd not gone home."

I couldn't blame him for that.

"When she called to tell you she was get-

ting married again did you ask her where and
when she'd gotten a divorce? Or why?''

"No, I never thought…" He frowned at me.
"Looking back now, I suppose I should have
asked her about it, but as I said, I knew they
were having problems so I just figured they'd
called it quits and she'd gotten a quickie Mexican one. Do you think she didn't get one at
all? I mean, even Caro wouldn't be that stupid."

"I could be wrong, but as she never told
anyone she'd ever been married at all, in fact
she flat-out told the pastor in the church where
she and Steven were married that she'd never
been married, she could very well not have
gotten a divorce. She may have figured no one
would ever find out. Daniel thought she was
dead and you weren't close."

"No, and I've wished…" he began in a
hard voice, stopped, sat for a moment with his
eyes closed, and started again more moder-
ately. "I wouldn't want anyone to die the way
she did but Caro had such a genius for getting
me into trouble of one kind or another I've
wished more than once that I'd never see her
again." He took a deep breath. "When she

was little she was forever getting into some kind of scrape I had to bail her out of, which was okay with me then. I was big brother taking care of my beautiful baby sister. But by the time she got into her teens her escapades were not only a lot more serious, they frequently got me into serious difficulties.'' He gave me a wry grin. ''Not a nice thing to say but I remember being glad to get away from her when I left for college.''

I stole a quick glance at my watch. It was after eleven. I didn't want to stop him as long as he was willing to talk, but he noticed me looking at the time.

''It's late and I never have told you what I wanted,'' he said with an apologetic little grimace. ''Daniel told me you're a private investigator. He advised me to hire you. I don't think that Lieutenant Morgan has the brains to find his way home, let alone find Caro's murderer, so I'd like you to work on it.''

It was a good thing I'd just dropped my napkin and bent over to pick it up. Not only was he lying—Daniel would never have told him anything of the kind—but more important, who the heck did he think he was, running Sam down that way? My face would have given me away for sure. As it was I had time to iron out my expression before I straightened up.

ELEVEN

I NEEDN'T HAVE WORRIED. He qualified his remark before I could open my mouth.

"That was a stupid thing to say," he said, shaking his head. "I must be more stressed than I realized. The lieutenant is obviously competent or he wouldn't be a lieutenant. I'm glad he didn't hear me." He grinned. "I'd hate to land in jail for bad-mouthing a police officer." He looked at his own watch. "It's getting late and I've still got the drive home, plus getting some work done for tomorrow. I wish you would consider my sharing the cost of your fees though. Daniel said it would be okay with him."

"I'll think about it," I said neutrally.

He held out his hand again, this time holding mine a little longer than necessary. "I'll call tomorrow. Will that be all right?"

I nodded. There were a number of people,

mostly couples, still sitting at tables as we walked out and I couldn't help noticing the admiring looks Roger got from the women. He was a handsome man, no doubt about that. Nice too. Or at least he seemed to be, but I long ago gave up on first impressions. I've been fooled too many times.

I PHONED SAM as soon as I got to the office the next morning. Something Roger said had come back to me in the middle of the night and I wanted to check with Sam. It had gone right over my head at the time, but now I was wondering. How had Sam known where to find Roger? Had Daniel told him, or was he in Caro's address book? And in either case, how had Roger known where to find Daniel?

Sam was surprisingly cooperative.

"I told him," Sam said in answer to my last question. "He was curious how I knew where he lived. Zimmer told me where Crawford was, or had been. Wasn't hard to find him. What difference does it make?"

"None, really. It's simply that he said he had minimal contact with his sister and I wondered if he was in her address book."

"I don't know whether he is or not; I haven't seen it. We got a warrant to check the house to see if the husband was in it, dead or injured, but not to search."

Ever since the O. J. case the police were being ver-r-y careful about that kind of thing.

"When did you talk to him? What time? He must have come right over to see Daniel. I wonder why?"

"When did you see Crawford?" he demanded. "I thought I told you—"

"Where was he? On vacation, I mean," I interrupted quickly before he could get started on his usual spiel. You'd think he'd get tired of telling me to stick to genealogy, but he never seemed to do so. "Hawaii?"

"Huh? Oh, no. Someplace down by Ocean Shores. Said he needed a rest."

Ocean Shores is a more or less local vacation spot for Seattlites. A fairly upscale oceanside resort community approximately three hours south and west of us in Gray's Harbor County. Roger hadn't said anything definite, but I'd thought from the sound of his conversation that he'd been farther away, Bermuda or Hawaii at least.

"Have you located Caro's husband?"

"Yes, he came home yesterday. We had a man watching the house. I talked to him then, and again a little while ago." He chuckled. "He has the perfect alibi. He was in jail in San Francisco, but see that you keep that to yourself. He works for a very conservative, old-line insurance company and he'd just as soon they learned from him where he was, and why. Not from some tabloid."

"Really? Why? Why was he in jail?"

Sam laughed again. "He was truly in the wrong place at the wrong time. Seems right after the speech he made on Friday night he and two of his friends decided to go down to Chinatown to see the sights. They went in and out of several cocktail bars and were just sitting down in what he described as a fancy nightclub when the place was raided by the narcotics squad. He spent most of the weekend in jail, along with assorted drunks, druggies, and other miscreants. He was most unhappy."

"Good grief. Didn't he tell them who he was? What he was doing in the place?"

"Of course he did, and probably at great length, but there were a hundred and thirty-two people in the Chinese nightclub and it took some time to process them all. I talked to the head of the squad myself this morning.''

''What did he say?''

''He said Gray was darn lucky he was the fifty-seventh guy processed and not the one hundred and thirty-first. Seems whoever was running drugs through the place was using tourists as regular carriers, so the narc boys checked everyone's story pretty thoroughly. Actually Gray was released Saturday afternoon, about three-thirty, but he waited for the other two men arrested with him before returning home. They all work for the same outfit, although not in the same office.''

''And then to come back to find his wife dead. Murdered. Poor guy.''

''Yeah.''

Sam still seemed willing to answer questions so I tried another one. ''Do you have any idea where it happened? Where she was killed?''

''According to the M.E.'s preliminary report this morning, it looks like she died right were she was found.''

"But…" I frowned.

"Uh-huh. No blood. He says she must have died just minutes before her throat was cut. Heart had already stopped so no blood was being pumped through the arteries. What blood there was on her clothes was drainage from the carotid."

"Yuck!" I shuddered. Sam loves to tell me that kind of detail in the hopes it will persuade me to quit snooping. It never works. Instead it just makes me angry. Angry at whoever committed the crime. Caro might not have been the sweetheart Daniel thought she was but that didn't make her the rotter Sara Lee made her out to be either. And nothing she was or did gave anyone the right to kill her.

"What did she die of if it wasn't getting her throat cut?" I asked, forcing myself to sound only superficially interested.

"Not sure, but it looks like alcohol poisoning. There was over eighteen ounces of un-metabolized booze in her stomach."

"Eighteen ounces! That's over two cups!"

"Right, enough to down a heavy drinker, and from what we've learned so far, she drank very little."

"What was it, do you know?"

"Nope, not specifically. Not so far. Apparently she had been eating and drinking for several hours previous to her death so, according to the doc, there were a number of components still present in her stomach. I don't know anything for sure yet. Doc Hazen is doing the autopsy, and asking him questions when he isn't ready to answer is like talking to the wall."

I nearly laughed aloud at Sam's aggrieved tone. Dr. Hazen had nothing on Sam when it came to refusing to talk when he didn't want to. But that did seem to be the end of what he was willing to tell me. We had a few minutes of personal conversation and then hung up.

"If you're through nattering away with that policeman, I have something more on Adam Parrick you might find interesting," Martha said, coming in and plopping herself down in one of the tangerine-colored chairs. "Tweaked *me,* anyway."

"Oh? What?"

"I built a quick family chart on him and discovered his grandson is Scott Meyer, your friend Sherry's favorite freelance photographer. He does the bulk of the magazine spreads she is in. Travels right with her on most of the shoots she does out of the country. He's thirty-five years old and apparently a model citizen. Now.'' She paused for emphasis. ''But...when he was twenty-two he was arrested for passing bogus cash. The charges were dismissed.''

''His grandfather is an engraver/printer, he got picked up for passing counterfeit money, and the charges were dismissed! You're kidding me!''

Martha rolled her eyes. ''The ways of the law are passing strange. Yes?''

TWELVE

"WHAT THE HECK happened? Where did he say he got it? Did it go to court? Was he held at all?"

Martha laughed, holding up her hands. "I thought that would get your attention. And I don't know—to all questions. All I've heard so far is the bare bones I just gave you. I called Carol Ann to ask if they had any form on Parrick and she happened to remember the case. She didn't have time to pull Meyer's sheet or anything."

I stared at her thoughtfully. "They may not have known Parrick was his grandfather, or what he did for a living, but still…I wonder who handled the case. It sounds absolutely crazy."

"She said she'd call back when she had more."

I doodled dollar signs on the pad in front of

me, scowling to myself. "Well, in the meantime see if you can set up an appointment for
me with Parrick to take a look at the La Tour
picture. This evening, if possible. Mrs. Barcasie seems to think he's the soul of virtue and
maybe he is, but I'd like to see it for myself.
And while you're at it, give the Honorable Violet a call too and ask her the name of the
young man she talked to in the museum. The
one who first told her about the La Tour."

"You think it was Meyer?"

"Possible. Dumb if it was, but dumber
things have happened."

Martha went out humming to herself. She
loves it when she can spring something like
that on me.

I decided I'd better get some work done on
a research project I was doing for a woman in
Astoria, Oregon. Her great-great-grandfather
had been one of the first permanent settlers in
Astoria, having arrived in 1827, a number of
years before the wagon trains even started
across the prairies. Mrs. Dobbe's genealogy
was well established before she came to me.
What she wanted me to do was to document
how the great-great had happened to arrive in

Astoria at all, why he stayed, and what he did during his lifetime. His parents, and grandparents, were farmers residing in upstate New York and there was no family record of how this member ended up in Astoria, which at that time was mostly a mud-floored fur-trading post out at the far end of nowhere.

It was a rather fun job. The great-great, whose name was Abner Macintosh, had come to Oregon with a group of fur traders who were loosely affiliated with John Jacob Astor's American Fur Company. Being an enterprising young man—he was seventeen at the time— he decided to go into the fur business himself. Beaver was plentiful and had a ready market. Ideal conditions for a teenage entrepreneur. To insure himself a steady source of pelts, he formed a liaison with a Palouse Indian woman from a village over closer to the mountains, near what is now the Idaho border. I had not been able to find any record of whether he actually married her or not, but I had documented two children, who were known as James and Charles Macintosh.

Setting himself up in opposition to Astor had apparently not been as smart a move as

Abner first thought. He went out of the fur trade within the year and into logging. He was mentioned in a number of documents pertaining to the treaty of 1846 that fixed the boundary of the Oregon territory at the 49th parallel, so by then he had become a respected member of the community, but I still hadn't been able to find out what he'd been doing in the meantime.

Astoria was, and is, a seaport, so it looked as if my next move was going to be checking the old shipping records. I couldn't seem to concentrate on Abner today though. My mind kept going back to Caro and the widely differing opinions people had of her. Daniel still thought she was a sweetheart; Mrs. Barcasie said she was a social-climbing tart. I wasn't sure what "tart" encompassed in the Hon. Violet's mind, but it didn't sound good. Sara Lee said she was a no-good tramp; Sarah Leah thought she was a sweet and generous person. Her brother said she was selfish and demanding. My own opinion, based on what I'd heard from others so far, was that she was narcissistic and obsessively self-centered. None of which was fuel for murder.

No one, other than Sara Lee who struck me as overexcitable, seemed to feel strongly enough about her to want to kill her, however. Even Caro's present husband, who might be justifiably angry when he found their marriage was bigamous—if it was—wouldn't have much of a motive for murder. It would be a lot easier just to leave her. Plus he had a pretty unassailable alibi.

Somebody obviously had a motive, or thought they did, but it certainly wasn't obvious to me. In my opinion the two most common motives for murder are fear and gain, neither of which seemed to apply. Caro had more to fear from others than anyone had to fear from her, or so it appeared at the moment anyway. She had no money to speak of so no one gained, financially, from her death.

I thought about that some more and was about to call Anna Carmine for an opinion when I heard her voice outside talking to Martha.

Anna is about fifty. She has the reputation of being an exceptionally good attorney, with few illusions regarding the majesty of the law. Tall and angular, she is a striking-looking woman without being really pretty. She keeps her black hair cut in a Liza Minnelli style, dresses in the very latest mode, and except for friends, has a general attitude of skepticism.

"Demary, how well do you know Roger Crawford?" she asked as I propped myself against the corner of Martha's desk.

"Not at all. I met him last night for the first time." I told her about Roger's call and our subsequent meeting at the Café Koffee.

She twined her fingers in her necklace, her face thoughtful. Her necklace, a Mandel, easily recognized by its beautiful hand-wound glass beads in brilliant shades of red, looked in imminent danger of being spilled all over the floor as she twisted them back and forth.

"Hmm, he certainly didn't leave me with the same impression you seem to have," she said when I finished. "But possibly I just misunderstood him. At any rate, he asked to see me this afternoon to discuss his position in regard to Caro Gray's death."

"What position?" Both Martha and I spoke at the same time.

Anna raised her eyebrows. "My thought exactly. However, he may have something in mind that I haven't thought of." She smiled, obviously doubting that possibility. "I told him to come tomorrow morning. I didn't have anything else to do tomorrow anyway."

With that she turned and walked back toward her office.

"That woman is dangerous," Martha remarked. "I do like the color of the dress she's wearing though."

I watched the flounce of her burnt-orange skirt swish around the corner of the hall. "You know, she might be on to something," I said. "I'm going to do a genealogy search on Caro's family."

"You already know most of it, don't you? Didn't Daniel say Caro and Roger had the same mother but different fathers, all of whom are now dead?"

"Yes, their mother married twice. Her first husband, Paul, Roger's father, was killed in Korea. Her second, Joe Peters, was Caro's father. And yes, Caro did tell him they were all dead. She also told Daniel that Roger was her only living relative, but given her track record, that may not be true. In fact, none of it may

be true. Which could be important. I think
maybe we'd better find out.''

And Caro hadn't been telling the truth, although I wasn't the one who traced Caro and
Roger's great-uncle, George Johnson. Martha
did. Carol Ann called just as I sat back down
in front of my computer and by the time I
finished talking to her Martha had not only
traced the uncle, she had the whole skinny on
him.

"How in the world did you get all this?" I
asked, flipping through the papers she handed
me.

"I'd like to tell you how smart I was but
actually it was pure accident,'' she said, sitting
down in one of the tangerine-colored chairs.
"I tried the Mormon data base and found
George right away, then I traced him to Alameda. He's lived there for fifty years. I've got
a mate who is on the paper down there so I
gave her a call. I know her from the old days,
when I was going to school at Berkeley. She
stayed in the Bay Area, and as it turned out
she's been doing some research on Johnson
for a feature her editor assigned her. He,
George Johnson I mean, is a well-known res-

ident of the city, contributes to a lot of chari-
ties, and used to be on any number of chari-
table boards. She faxed me all the bumf.''

''You said, used to be. Is he dead?''

''No, he just doesn't get around as much
nowadays. He's ninety-five. The feature is in
the way of a birthday tribute.''

THIRTEEN

"And that ain't all I found," Martha said, using one of our bad grammar catchphrases.

"There's more?"

"A proper beauty that Caro is, or was," Martha said. "And I'm not referring to her looks. Caro and Roger have a whole carload, in fact a busload, of relatives. None of them close, but they certainly exist, and here's the bomb. Your friend Sherry Hall is related to both Roger and Caro."

"Sherry? Impossible. How could they all be related?"

"I'm not sure of the exact, I have to look at the chart, but I think they are first cousins four times removed. And I certainly doubt that any of them knew it."

"You got that right, as far as Sherry is concerned anyway. She would have told me. What's the connection?"

"Roger, Caro, and Sherry all have the same great-great-grandmother, Alana Vane. Vane's daughter, Susan, married Carl Johnson and had two children, George and Margaret. George is Roger and Caro's great-uncle, Margaret their grandmother. Alana, the great-great, had a sister, Bertha; her daughter, Wanda, had a son—"

"Never mind, I'll take your word for it. I still can't follow the cousin removes without the chart in front of me. Where do they live?"

"All over the place, but the most I've been able to trace so far are in New England."

"Good grief. The next thing will be they're all related to *you*."

"Not likely. I don't have that kind of trashy relatives. Except for Sherry. I wouldn't mind claiming her."

"Sherry did tell me once that she had some cousins in Boston," I said, trying to bring the conversation back to mind. "It seems to me she mentioned them a couple of years ago, said she'd never met them but was going to give them a call the next time she was in New York for a show. I'll have to ask her when she gets back. What day is today? Tuesday? She said she would be back on Thursday. I'll try her then. Did you get Mrs. Barcasie?"

"Yes, but I think you guessed wrong there. It wasn't Scott. The helpful grandson was Dennis Meyer, Scott's fifteen-year-old son."

"That's interesting." I stopped for a minute, thinking. "But it doesn't get me much forwarder, as the saying goes. I just talked to Carol Ann and she—"

"Before you get to her," Martha interrupted, "think about this. Terry, my friend in Alameda, told me the reason for the birthday tribute is that Mr. Johnson, who has never married, recently informed a group of Alameda businessmen that he intends to make out a will leaving his assets in three parts. The largest portion would go to his two closest relatives, the next lot would be divided equally among his more distant kin, and the third cut was going to the city of Alameda to build a plaza in his memory. Which to me suggests we're talking a lot of money."

"Oh, my! I hope his lawyer had him list the exact kin by name or the probate will outlast the century, and then some."

"Uh-huh. According to what I've done so

far on his chart the two closest are, or were, Caro and her brother, but the more distant could include your friend Sherry's family. Also, when he said closest, he may not have meant by blood. He could easily have meant closest to him either in distance, living next door or something, or closest to his heart.''

"Be interesting to know how much money is involved. If it's a lot I suppose it could be the motive. Money is always a prime one. But it's so farfetched, and you'd have to know the exact terms of the will to know if anyone benefited from Caro's death.'' I frowned, shaking my head. "Roger never mentioned him; in fact something he said gave me the idea that he believed Caro was the only relative he had, so he may never have known the man. I suppose some avid Alameda booster could have offed him for the plaza, but if your friend is right he hasn't even made out this will yet. Despite his age it doesn't sound like he's in any imminent danger of departing this earth anyway.''

"Plus, he may change his mind,'' Martha said, shrugging. "And Roger may be as big a liar as his sister, who knows? So what did Carol Ann have to say?''

I grinned. "She said if she was going to keep doing our work for us she wanted better returns than an occasional cup of coffee. One of us had better take her to lunch. And, guess what, Dave Benson was the detective in charge of the case but Jake Allenby also worked it. I called him after I talked to Carol Ann but he couldn't add much to what she'd already told me."

Jake was a sometimes date of mine and he was usually more than willing to tell me anything he knew about a case. He and Sam were good friends but ridiculously jealous of the time I spent with the other. Although why they should be I never have figured out. I didn't owe either one of them the time of day.

"So what did they have to say?" Martha asked.

"Scott's story, which checked out, was that he got the twenty when he cashed his paycheck the same as he always did in a well-known place out on Fifteenth. Ship's Restaurant. It's not there anymore but I remember it well. The food was good and it was always swamped on Fridays because they were willing to cash payroll checks. The cashier named a number of people who had given him a twenty that afternoon but admitted there were probably a dozen more that he couldn't remember. There was even the possibility that it was in the money the restaurant got from the bank. So that was that."

"Did Jake know Parrick was his grandfather, and what he did for a living?"

"Jake says not, but it was so many years ago he wasn't sure. He said he'd talk to Dave as soon as he got the chance and see if he remembered anything else."

"Dead end then," Martha said, getting up. "Plus it was so long ago it doesn't matter anyway."

I sat and thought about that after she'd gone out. It was a long time ago, but if the twenty was some of Parrick's work I didn't think a minor scare such as that one would have stopped production. And if Scott went out of the country everytime Sherry did, he was in a perfect position to get rid of any amount of counterfeit. Certainly in Western Europe merchants were more than willing to take U.S. greenbacks. And there were undoubtedly plenty of crooks over there as well as over here willing to buy it at a discount.

It would probably be easy enough to get it through Customs too. Sherry had told me once that she went to Paris so much she hardly had to slow down going through. Most of the Customs inspectors knew her by sight and just waved her on her way. And they very likely knew Scott just as well, as he nearly always accompanied her.

None of which had anything to do with the La Tour but it was certainly going to make me take a harder-than-ever look at the thing.

Martha's information about the great-uncle sounded a bit more interesting, regardless of whether he had already made out the will he'd spoken of or not. Or any will at all for that matter. Although people with that kind of money were usually pretty careful about keeping their will up-to-date. If the man was worth a great deal of money and Caro was one of his closest relatives, she could have inherited a bundle. The question was, who would that bundle go to now? Roger? Daniel? Steven? And more important, did whoever killed her know about George and the proposed will?

FOURTEEN

PARRICK'S HOUSE WAS a charming old remodeled farmhouse on a three-acre plot in the Mountlake Terrace area. Most of the furniture was old and worn but showed a lot of TLC, as did the knickknacks on the tables and mantelpiece, some of which looked like they might be antiques. Everything shone with polish. There were several very nice paintings on the walls. He said his grandfather had purchased the house in the early 1930s when it was considered too far away from Seattle to be worth much. When the surrounding countryside was just that, countryside, and before Mountlake Terrace, as such, was even thought about. Now he was surrounded by multihundred-thousand-dollar homes set on one-hundred-foot lots.

"I'll bet your neighbors are green with

envy," I said, looking out the window at his orchard and garden.

"No, surprisingly, they aren't," he said in his pleasant voice. "In fact a number of them have told me how much they enjoy seeing the orchard in bloom and how glad they are that I haven't cut the place up into lots and sold them off." He grinned mischievously. "Of course I don't tell them I couldn't cut it up if I wanted to."

"You can't?" I said, surprised. "Why not?"

"Some kind of environmental thing. But I don't mind, I like it just as it is. And there's plenty of room for the grandchildren and their friends to come. I like that too."

Adam Parrick was a tall stooped man with thinning hair and a gentle manner. Not the sort of person one would associate with any kind of crime. His wife, a darling little butterball of a woman, was as pleasant as he and tried to serve me coffee and cake. I had a hard time persuading her I'd just eaten. Fortunately, Adam seemed to understand and shooed her out of the room.

The Georges de La Tour, hung in the dining

room now, was a beautiful picture and as far as I could tell appeared genuine. Which certainly didn't mean it was. I knew next to nothing about seventeenth-century painting and had never heard of Georges de La Tour before the Hon. Violet walked into my office. However, that wasn't my problem. Mrs. Barcasie had already hired an expert to authenticate it, which he would do as soon as I documented the provenance. All I was supposed to do was make sure it wasn't stolen, or otherwise illegal, and after talking to Parrick for less than a half hour I'd pretty well changed my mind about him.

He told me quite a bit about the painting but admitted it was all stuff he'd looked up in the library after learning the picture might be worth something. According to him, La Tour painted several of what were called "the cardsharp pictures." One, entitled *The Cheat with the Ace of Diamonds,* belonged to the Louvre, another to the Kimbell Museum. They weren't exactly the same but they were very similar. There was no known record of how many pictures La Tour had painted in all, but he was

known to have done several on this same
theme.

He gave me copies of all the papers he had
relating to the purchase of the picture but said
he didn't know anything about them personally. He was a year old when his grandfather
brought the picture home and didn't remember
even seeing it until he was eight or ten. As he
said, anything he knew about the picture was
either what he'd been told or what he'd read.

He smiled at me. "I do remember seeing it
quite often though, because it hung in the attic
and Gran always sent us up there to play
whenever the weather was bad. We were a
noisy bunch."

"You say, we. Who was we? I understood
you were an only child," I said.

"I am and my father was also, but I had a
host of friends, and so did he. All with big
families, so I had plenty of playmates. I've
been lucky that way," he said in his gentle,
unassuming way.

I quite liked Mr. Parrick and would be sorry
if I found out he wasn't as honest as he appeared. We talked a few minutes longer, shook
hands, and I said good-bye. He walked me out

to my car and stood in the driveway until I turned the corner. He seemed to be a really nice man and I certainly did like their house. It was a lot like mine in some ways.

I inherited mine from my great-aunt. She had no children and had told me years before she died that she was leaving it to me in her will because I was the only one who had ever appreciated it. I have loved the place ever since I was small. It looks like a Victorian wedding cake. Three stories high, tall, and narrow, with acres of gingerbread trim, scalloped and diamond-shaped shingles, ten-foot ceilings and hardwood plank floors. It has wraparound porches on all three floors with hand-turned railings. It also has a few drawbacks, such as costing a small fortune to heat, has only one bathroom, and carries a horrendous mortgage. I still think it's wonderful though, and always pull into my drive with a sense of pleasure.

Tonight Joey was sitting on my porch looking like a cat who has cornered a tasty-sized mouse. An expression I always distrust. It means he has been snooping again.

He jumped up and came over to the car before I had shut the motor off. "Got something interesting," he said, leaning in the window.

"Joey, you haven't been putting yourself in harm's way, have you?" I asked sharply. With Joey, "something interesting" could be anything from the most trivial to having found an eyewitness to the murder itself.

"Now don't go giving me attitude, Demary," he said, raising his eyebrows. "I only been talking to one of my ladies, name of Mrs. Taylor. She found the body, you know."

"Oh," I said, backing down. Joey was a great favorite with elderly ladies. He knew a number of them whom he called on at least once a week, running errands, making small repairs around their houses, and sometimes buying their groceries for them.

"Did she tell you something about Caro that she didn't tell the police?" I asked, my voice rising in alarm.

"No," he said regretfully. "But she does know something and she will tell you. So c'mon and we'll go see what it is." He went around and got in on the passenger side. "You know where she lives?"

I nodded, backing out of the drive. "Why didn't she tell you?"

He shook his head. "I don't know. But when I told her I worked with you on lots of your cases she said she'd tell you about it, whatever it is."

I gave him a sharp look at the "working with me" part but he ignored it and went on. "Probably something she thinks I'm too young to hear." He sighed. "I keep telling her this is the nineties, anything goes, but she don't buy it."

That amused me. It took a strong will to withstand Joey's powers of persuasion.

Joey took me into the house and introduced me to Mrs. Taylor in a surprisingly formal way, then excused himself with a remark about having to check on the outside garden faucet.

"He is a dear," she said with an affectionate smile at his retreating back. "He probably thinks I think he's too young to hear, but that isn't it at all. I just wanted to make sure you got it right." She paused. "That certainly sounds as if I know something momentous, doesn't it? I don't, but come along with me and I'll show you."

I followed her through a dining room complete with a beautiful old claw-footed table and matching china cabinet full of sparkling cut glass, and into a bedroom at the back of the house.

She went over to the window and motioned to me to come closer. "As you can see I have a very shallow backyard and so does the house across the alley. Steven Gray's house. The window on the left is their kitchen. I think the one on the right is a guest bedroom. There used to be several trees in the yard which gave them more privacy but they became overgrown and Steven had them cut down."

She did have a completely open view of the back of the Gray house.

"I don't make a habit of watching my neighbors," she went on in a wry tone, "but on the other hand I don't go out of my way to not watch either. In any case, Caro took so few precautions to conceal her behavior I'm surprised the whole neighborhood didn't know about her carrying on. The alley is fairly well lit at night; there's a light on Steven's garage

as well as the one next door, and as you can
see, the way my bed is positioned I have an
excellent view of the whole area. I could see
Caro and her boyfriends very clearly when
they brought her home in the wee small
hours.''

FIFTEEN

"HER BOYFRIEND?" I wasn't too surprised she'd had one, just that she'd apparently been so obvious the neighbors knew all about it. But as I'd observed before, she wasn't very sharp.

"Well, I suppose they'd be called something different nowadays," Mrs. Taylor said, her eyes snapping. "But they were male and they were certainly friendly. You know, there's a great deal of difference between love and...and other things, and one doesn't necessarily include the other."

"Which one?" I asked, intrigued.

"Either one. But I'm not sure poor Caro knew the difference. At any rate they parted with affectionate kisses. To say the least. She always jumped out of the car, ran around, and leaned in the driver's-side window for a last good-bye."

About that time it dawned on me that Mrs. Taylor was using plural pronouns all the time, not just when she included Caro. "You said they, do you mean she had more than one, ah, friend?"

"Well, I would certainly think so. Or he was extremely wealthy. I seldom saw the same car more than twice or maybe three times. And they were usually expensive cars. Cadillacs, Chryslers, a Saab, even a BMW once. I'm not up on the latest models anymore but my husband talked cars constantly so I am familiar with most types."

"Have you told the police?"

"No. They didn't ask me anything so I didn't tell them anything." She turned away from the window and looked at me thoughtfully. "The truth is, I didn't really want to talk to them about her. I felt sorry for the girl. She was so foolish. Steven is a very nice man and she didn't treat him very nicely but one just doesn't want to speak ill of the dead. And I thought they would catch whoever was responsible right away. But now... Well, Joey convinced me I should talk to you."

I stared out at the alleyway, running my fingers through my hair. "No, Caro didn't treat her husband well, and I'm beginning to think you're right. She was a foolish woman. She treated her first husband shabbily too and he's a great guy. But that is no reason to kill her."

"Of course not. But some women are like that. They never know when they are well off. Or they are so insecure they need constant reassurance that they are attractive, that other men are still interested in them."

"Did this go on all the time? Why didn't Steven ever catch her if she was so open about her dalliances?"

"Oh no. She only met these men when he was out of town." Mrs. Taylor sighed. "She was really quite dull-witted about it. She seemed to think no one would spot what she was doing. When Steven went on a trip, which he had to do frequently, he took his suitcase to the office when he left the house in the morning. I know this because I was great friends with Nancy, his first wife, and she told me so. And anytime he was carrying a suitcase when he left, Caro would call a cab when she went out later that same evening. And then I'd see her return in the early hours. Any other time, when Steven was not going away, she used her own car when she went out.''

"And I suppose everyone in the neighborhood eventually caught on.''

"Very likely. I know Violet Barcasie did. Because of the way her house is situated she looks straight down the alley and the car lights shone right in her bedroom window. She lives up there on the cross street.''

"Do you think you would recognize any of the men?''

"No. They always came in from my left, so the drivers were on the opposite side of the car from me. I never saw them clearly.''

We went back through the dining room to where I could see Joey sitting on the porch steps waiting for me.

"Thank you for telling me, Mrs. Taylor. I don't know that it will help my client but it can't hurt.''

"Will you tell the police?''

"Yes, I'll tell the lieutenant in charge of the case, but again, I don't know that it will help him any. He'll undoubtedly try to find out who these men were but if she always returned the way you say it doesn't sound as if anyone in the neighborhood will be able to identify them, so they may be hard to find.'' I thought for a moment. ''You didn't by any chance see them Saturday night?''

''No. I would have told the policeman that. You might ask Donna White, across from Caro's house, if she saw Caro go out on Saturday, but I rather doubt she did. Go out, I mean.''

''Oh? Why not?''

''Caro had a terrible head cold. I saw her in the alley late Friday evening emptying the trash and spoke to her for a moment. Just a neighborly 'hello' but I couldn't help noticing how wretched she looked. Her nose was red, her eyes were swollen, and her throat was absolutely raw. She could hardly speak, she was so hoarse. As vain as she was I don't think she'd have wanted any of her gentlemen friends to see her.''

I grinned. ''You're probably right.'' I started for the front door, then turned back. ''You said one of the cars was a Saab. Do you remember the color?''

She thought a moment. ''Oh, yes. That was

one of the recent ones. It was white, or cream-colored.''

Daniel drove a white Saab.

WEDNESDAY MORNING was bright and sunny but I didn't exactly feel a match for the weather. I pulled on an old pair of jeans that were faded almost white and a T-shirt emblazoned with the Seahawks' logo. It was Nora's day to come do the house and that meant I had to get up earlier than I wanted in order to scurry around and pick up the kitchen or my clothes, or whatever Nora considers my duty, not hers. I inherited Nora with the house; she was working for my aunt at the time and agreed to give me a ''try,'' but she is definitely not everyone's idea of the ideal housekeeper. She refuses to do what she calls ''pick up after me'' and has been known to mop around a towel I left on the bathroom floor. And leave me a sharp note about my slovenly habits! On the other hand she not only does the windows and keeps the place spotlessly clean, she even vacuums the porches.

But mostly I was not happy about that white Saab. As someone had said to me recently, just because Daniel was a friend didn't make him innocent of any wrongdoing.

I pushed the thought to the back of my mind when I got to the office, and after having a cup of coffee with Martha, went to work on the La Tour thing. I had Martha check if any of the people or places on the documents Parrick and Violet had given me had either fax numbers or website addresses, and then went to work composing letters to the various German government offices that might have art records. The name of the art gallery owner where the painting had been purchased was Benjamin Golder, a common Jewish name. Given the year the painting was purchased, I doubted if I'd be able to find any trace of him or his family but it was worth a try, so I framed a letter to the authorities in Israel too.

By the time I finished all those, and a letter to the Louvre in Paris, it was after eleven, so I decided to go downtown and see if I could persuade Sam to take me to lunch. I thought of trying to bribe him with Mrs. Taylor's information but decided against that ploy. He'd ruin my lunch, if he even agreed to take me, by lecturing me the whole time. I'd tell him but I'd wait until after we'd eaten.

I changed my mind when I was halfway to town and ended up going to one of my favorite places, the Pike Street Market. I love the sights and sounds of the big open-air marketplace—the smell of flowers, fresh seafood, and exotic spices. I even enjoy the vendors' harsh voices as they call out their wares, and seeing their colorful piles of crisp fresh vegetables and fruit. I ate a solitary lunch at one of the old market restaurants that have big windows facing Elliot Bay. The view was as spectacular as usual, with Washington State ferryboats churning in and out of the Colman Dock trailing their white foam skirts, sailboats skip-dancing across the choppy water, and tiny little tugs towing long strings of barges or rafts of logs in from the Strait of Juan de Fuca. In the far distance the snow-topped peaks of the Olympic Mountains traced a jagged line across the sky.

I was dawdling over a last half cup of coffee when I saw a white Saab pull up in one of the parking spaces on Western Avenue, below the market. The driver got out and locked his door, turned, and came two steps in my direction before moving out of sight between the other cars.

Two steps were enough. Even at that distance I recognized him easily. It was Roger Crawford, Caro's half-brother.

SIXTEEN

TWO POSSIBLE SUSPECTS driving white Saabs? That was stretching the bounds of coincidence. The Saab is not all that common a car.

I left my old Toyota parked where it was and took the free shuttle bus down First Avenue, got off at Pioneer Square, and walked up Cherry to Sam's office. He was on the phone when I went in so I wandered over to the window and watched the people in the little plaza across the street. A circle of pots filled with bright yellow flowers surrounded the magnolia in the center of the little square. A couple of young women were sitting on the steps eating bag lunches and enjoying the sun.

"Okay, Demary, what have you gotten yourself into now?" Sam asked as he hung up.

"For Pete's sake, what gives you the idea I've gotten myself into anything?" I asked, in a milder tone than I usually used when re-

sponding to an opening like that. The white
Saabs were bugging me. I liked both of those
guys and I hated to tell Sam about the one
Mrs. Taylor had seen but I didn't see any help
for it. I didn't have the time nor the manpower
to hunt for the drivers. He did, and one of
them could well be Caro's killer.

"How did you happen to be talking to Mrs.
Taylor?" he asked when I finished.

"Why shouldn't I talk to her?" I demanded.

He sighed. "I wish... Never mind. Anyway,
I'm beginning to think the Gray woman
wasn't playing with a full deck. We haven't
been able to find any record of her filing for
divorce anywhere, she pulled that plane stunt,
she was using a phony Social Security number, and if Mrs. Taylor is right she was seeing
a regular troop of men whenever her husband
was out of town. She must have been off her
nut."

"What about her Social Security number?
How, when..."

"She was working as a receptionist for a
small title company when she met Gray. That
was how she met him. They worked in the
same building. She didn't work there long and

had already quit by the time the title company found out she'd given them an incorrect number, so they just forgot about it. But they did remember when we talked to them.''

"What in the world would she do something like that for?"

"No idea. Except that of course if Zimmer, or anyone else, tried to trace her through the Social Security office they wouldn't have been able to do so.''

I paced back and forth, thinking. "It sounds almost as if she was on the run from something, or somebody.''

"I suppose she was, in a way, but she hadn't been involved in anything criminal. The INS has her prints on file because of Zimmer's job and if she'd ever been arrested for anything we'd have gotten a report by now. She could have been on the run from somebody with a record but I doubt it. Like I said, I honestly think some of her circuits were jammed.''

I had to agree. "Why don't you see if KIRO or KING TV will do a story on her with a picture?" I asked. "Maybe someone saw her Saturday night with the guy and will call in.''

He shrugged. "Good idea, except we don't have a picture. We asked Gray but he says she had a regular phobia about having her picture taken. He doesn't even have a snap."

"Maybe Roger...oh, wait, I've got one. Daniel gave it to me. Come to think of it though he did say it was the only one he had and to be careful of it. It's in the top drawer of my desk. Have a black-and-white pick it up. I'll call Martha to get it out."

After we had that taken care of and talked a while, I left, or started to. Walking out Sam's door I spotted Jake down the hall and called to him to wait. I wanted to ask him if he had looked up Scott's arrest sheet. He turned and gave me a welcoming smile that suddenly broadened. I saw his eyes go beyond me and realized without turning that Sam had followed me out the door for some reason.

"Jake, I need to talk to you," I said.

"Sure," he said, starting back toward me.

I turned slightly, bringing Sam into my line of sight too. He was looking at Jake, hard, and Jake, by now, was beaming at me with as adoring a smile as I'd ever seen. In fact, one

I'd never seen on his face before. Jake and I are good friends, nothing else.

The end of Sam's nose was turning an interesting shade of puce. Within the hierarchy of the department he was Jake's superior but at least he had sense enough not to try that on. Instead he just glared. The two of them were ridiculous, both grown men, eyeing each other like a couple of tomcats facing off over an old fish bone.

I couldn't help it—I burst out laughing.

Sam turned, stiff-backed, and returned to his office. He closed the door quietly. Very quietly.

Jake scowled. "Now look what you've gotten me into, Demary. What do you want, anyway?"

"I didn't get you into anything," I retorted, still grinning. "You did it yourself and on purpose too."

He had the grace to look chagrined. He has a quirky sense of humor sometimes. I was tempted to tell him both he and Sam acted like a couple of fools but didn't think the comment would go over too well when I was asking a favor.

"All I wanted was to ask if you'd talked to Dave Benson," I said mildly.

"Yeah, I talked to him, and as far as he's concerned Scott got the counterfeit bill in change somewhere just like he said. And no, he didn't know his grandfather was an engraver but it wouldn't have made any difference in his thinking. Or at least so he said. He was in charge of the case, I wasn't, and to tell the truth I don't actually remember it at all. I think I would if I'd had any suspicions at the time."

I didn't agree with him but I didn't argue. I have a built-in distrust of coincidence, and there were already too many of them bubbling around the La Tour. I still thought there was a very good chance Scott was passing counterfeit in Europe but I didn't have a scrap of proof, so until I did I didn't have a prayer of convincing either one of these two guys.

I WENT BACK UP to the market for my car, stopping first at DeLaurentis market for sourdough bread, olives, homemade mayonnaise, and some of their thin sliced Italian ham, and then to a couple of vegetable stalls for a head of Bibb lettuce, bok choy, a red onion, and some tiny zucchini squash. Hopefully I'd feel guilty enough after eating the ham to go to my aerobics class in the morning.

It was still only three-thirty though, so I went back to the office and after catching Martha up-to-date went to work on my computer setting up a new data base on Caro's murder. I listed everyone who had any connection, however remote, with her and then cross-referenced them by category—relative, neighbor, friend, etc.—to both Caro and to each other. I transferred everything I had in the file I'd started on Monday and then keyboarded in everything I knew, or had heard about, or been told by each one as I went along, listing both Saras, Sara Lee's brother-in-law, whose name it took me a while to dredge out of my memory, Mrs. Taylor, Mrs. Barcasie, the receptionist at the health club, Raphael at the hair salon, and anyone else I could think of. It made an imposing file but it didn't get me anywhere. At least not at the moment. But one thing did strike me. Although I had Steven Gray in the mix I didn't know anything about him other than where he'd spent the weekend. I needed to do something about that.

Martha had gone home sometime before. It was nearly six, which I thought might be a good time to catch Steven Gray at home. His number rang four times and I'd about decided I was wrong about finding him in when he picked up. I introduced myself, expressed my condolences, and told him why I wanted to see him.

He hesitated for a moment and then said he'd be going out for dinner later but if I came over right away he'd be glad to talk to me.

I thanked him for his patience and said I'd be right there.

SEVENTEEN

STEVEN GRAY WAS a very handsome man with dark hair streaked with silver at his temples, brown eyes, and a gracious manner. He and Caro must have been a striking couple when together.

He greeted me courteously and escorted me on into the big living room to the right of the hall. It was furnished in strong colors, dark reds and blues with navy drapes at the windows, stark white walls, and bright modernistic pictures. The effect was attractive but not particularly restful. I wondered who was responsible for the decor, Caro, or Steven's first wife? I was glad I'd gone home and changed to a raw linen pants suit before I came. This was not a room for jeans and a T-shirt.

Gray waved me to a chair upholstered in a satin striped maroon fabric and then asked, ''Can I get you anything, before I sit down?

Coffee? A glass of wine? I have some very nice Gewurztraminer already chilled.''

"Yes, I'd love a glass of that,'' I said.

He went behind the built-in bar that separated the front room from the dining room and took a bottle out of the refrigerated wine rack alongside some shelves holding an assortment of glasses. He opened and poured, put the two glasses on a silver tray, and brought them over to the coffee table.

After I'd taken a sip of mine—it was very good wine—he sat down.

"Now tell me how I can help,'' he said, giving me a pleasant smile.

For a man who had lost his wife just three days previously, and under particularly gruesome circumstances, he certainly appeared cool, calm, and collected. But then, everyone deals with their losses in different ways.

"I'm not sure where to start,'' I said. ''I guess by explaining that Caro's former husband, Daniel Zimmer, is a friend of mine and he has asked me to find out what I can about her death. I know you didn't know about him before, but have the police told you who he is?''

"Yes. I haven't met him, but a Lieutenant Morgan has told me Caro was married to him previously, when she lived in New York. Also that they can't locate any record of a divorce, but I don't find that surprising. Mexican divorce records aren't exactly well kept."

"Caro told you she divorced Daniel in Mexico?" I had a hard time swallowing that in view of Sara Lee's description of their wedding certificate.

He shook his head. "No, but I know she spent some time in El Paso and Juarez so she must have gotten it then. I certainly think so. Whatever else she might have been, Caro wasn't a fool about things like that. But for some reason she always…uh… Well, to be blunt about it, and I suppose that's the only way we'll ever know what happened, Caro wasn't always truthful."

That was an understatement if I ever heard one.

"She was totally unrealistic, a dreamer. She lived in a make-believe world," he went on in a flat, unemotional tone. "Everything she had anything to do with had to be beautiful, wonderful, exciting. She lived life as if it were a soap opera, a TV series, or a movie, where nothing she did was ever wrong or deceitful in anyway, simply a new adventure. I didn't, of course, realize this when I married her, but it didn't take me long to find out.''

That fit with what Daniel had told me about her being disappointed when she found out he didn't have what she considered an exciting job.

"Sara Lee told me you were married in her church and—''

He made an impatient gesture, interrupting me. "Oh, yes, the wedding certificate. That was so typical of Caro. She undoubtedly wanted the certificate to be perfect so she couldn't say she'd been married before. She never told me either and for probably the same reason.'' He looked at me thoughtfully. "I'm not trying to make excuses for Caro. The lieutenant told me about the plane, that Zimmer thought she was dead, or said he did. And if true, it was a terrible thing for her to have done. But that was what she was like. What else can I say?''

I took another sip of wine. "You say you

soon realized that she wasn't what you'd thought. Were you having problems?''

He gave me a rather hard look, then shrugged. ''I suppose that is something you need to know. But no, we didn't have any problems. I simply began to realize what she was like. And on the whole I didn't care. I never was as madly in love with her as people thought, but I did love her and she was the perfect wife for me. I'm in a very competitive business and I needed a wife like Caro. She was very decorative, a good hostess, and knew how to play up to the right people.''

That was about as chill an epitaph as I've ever heard. I didn't think I liked this man.

''Did you entertain a lot?'' I asked.

''Yes, it's part of my job. Another good thing about Caro was that although she'd take a social drink at a party she never drank more than one and almost never when we were alone. The only alcohol she actually liked was gin and she had developed an allergy to it so she rarely even had a single martini.''

''What did it do to her?''

''Oh, nothing fatal; she simply got a head-ache almost immediately, so she left it alone.''

"Mrs. Taylor, the lady across the alley, said Caro had a terrible cold on Friday. Had she been sick long? I mean, could it have been anything more serious than a cold? Could she have left the house Saturday night to seek medical help? To go to a clinic or an emergency room?"

He thought for a moment, sipping his wine. "I doubt it. She'd had a cold for several days and was still fighting it when I left Friday morning but she was beginning to feel much better. In fact she said something about going to change the sheets on our bed. She had been sleeping in the spare room for a couple of nights because she was so restless."

"Frankly, my problem is figuring out what she was doing outside at that time of night," I said neutrally. "Feeling as she did, it was unlikely that she'd go out to dinner and she wasn't with any of her friends. Or at least none that the police have located yet."

He got up and paced over to one of the windows. In a moment he turned back, looking, for the first time, like a man who had lost a beloved wife. "I don't know," he said in a voice barely above a whisper. "I don't know.

She very rarely went out at all when I was gone, and why that night, I can't even guess.''

He suddenly looked so miserable I hated to ask him anything else, but so far I hadn't learned much so I steeled myself and asked, ''Had she been at all different lately? Moody, short-tempered, absentminded, nervous, anything? I suppose those sound like idiotic questions, but so far neither I nor the police, as far as I know, have even a hint of a motive for her death, and the only thing I can think of is the possibility of something outside her life bothering her.''

''Outside her life?'' He frowned, puzzled. ''I don't know what you mean. Outside her life how?''

''I guess I should have said something outside her life with you. For instance, something she'd learned or been told about an old friend, man or woman, or a relative. Or something from her past that was catching up with her.'' With the last, of course, I was referring to Daniel. I wondered if he'd known, or knew now, that Caro's ex had moved in practically next door.

'No, she'd been the same as always.''

"Had she done anything different than usual?"

"No, and Miss Jones, I've already answered these questions several times. For the police." He hesitated, looking at his watch. "And I think I've answered about all I can for you."

"Of course." I got up and put my glass back on the tray. There was no use pushing him, he had himself too well under control. "I hope I haven't upset you. I certainly didn't mean to."

"No, it's just that I..." The words trailed off as he escorted me to the hall and opened the door.

"Thanks for talking to me." I held out my hand.

He shook it briefly and then suddenly tightened his hold, frowning. "Wait. She *had* done something different. I'd forgotten. Caro didn't like to travel. That's why she didn't go with me when I went out of town. She could have. A lot of wives did. She never wanted to. But just two weeks ago she bought a set of expensive luggage. And a bunch of new clothes that were not her usual. You know, the kind of clothes specifically designed for traveling.

Skirt, jacket, pants, shorts, several kinds of tops. Those wrinkle-free things that have six or eight pieces in different shades of the same color that can be worn in several different combinations. When I asked her about them she said she was going to go with me the next time I went somewhere interesting. I'd forgotten about that.''

When he went somewhere interesting? I wondered if that was what she really had in mind. Or if Caro was getting ready to do another flit. And if so, with whom?

EIGHTEEN

I ATE MY Italian ham and other goodies sitting at the small table in front of my kitchen window that overlooks the backyard. I don't like grubbing in the dirt, so the backyard is mostly paved with quarry tile. Several big pots filled with bright, easy-growing annuals sit here and there between three ornamental trees in big pottery tubs. Plus there is a small raised fishpond in the center with water lilies floating on the surface. I put a half dozen tiny little goldfish in the pond a couple of years ago. They have grown to the size of small trout despite the pet shop owner telling me they wouldn't survive outside. He also told me I had to feed them regularly but I forget most of the time and they seem to do very well on their own self-caught diet of gnats and other bugs that come for a drink.

The various facets of Caro's personality—

or maybe behavior was a better word—went round and round in my head as I ate. Everyone had a totally different picture of her stored in their memory. I tended to think Steven had the right one. He wasn't sentimental and what he'd said of her fit the facts, or what facts I had.

I thought about that for a while and changed my mind about one thing. There were a couple of constants. Almost everyone felt sorry for her to one degree or another and no one credited her with much intelligence, but after mulling over all I'd heard about her I came to a slightly different conclusion. She may have done things that others didn't agree with but it had taken considerable smarts to disappear the way she had and to get away with it for so long. She had certainly pulled the wool over a great many eyes for a significant period of time. I wondered if the gin allergy had been some kind of a cover-up too. She had definitely consumed plenty of it the night she died. Carol Ann had called yesterday afternoon and told Martha the alcohol contents of Caro's stomach had been primarily gin.

The only really witless bit of behavior I

knew of concerned the men Mrs. Taylor saw
her with, and even that might not be what it
seemed, although at the moment I couldn't see
what else it could be other than cheating on
her husband.

Some of the things she'd done, such as the
vandalism in Daniel's backyard, were childish
rather than wicked. And in that case she'd undoubtedly been panicked. In fact, by the time
I finished my dinner I was beginning to almost
feel sorry for the woman, in addition to her
being murdered, that is.

The one thing I simply could not get a han-
dle on was motive. No one had any real reason
for killing her. She was no threat to anyone,
no one had anything to gain from her death,
and other than Sara Lee, no one seemed to feel
very strongly about her one way or the other.
Not even Daniel, and certainly not Steven
Gray, who, to my mind, acted almost un-
touched by his wife's death.

I GOT TO THE OFFICE early the next morning
and went to work keyboarding in my meeting
with Steven, plus what conclusions I'd drawn,
and a list of questions I'd thought of when I

woke up in the middle of the night. I do some of my best thinking when I wake up like that.

When Martha came in I brought her up to date again. Like Anna Carmine, she wears clothes beautifully and today had on a great outfit. Very dark purple tunic over a purple, green, violet, and maroon-splashed skirt made of a silky material that swirled around her ankles when she walked. We kicked my meeting with Steven around for a while but she couldn't come up with a reasonable motive for him either.

"As far as I can see the woman was not around the twist by any means," Martha said judiciously. "Just so self-centered she never gave a thought to anyone else, but I can't see that kind of thing as a motive for killing her."

"Me neither. So I still haven't heard anything else that even suggests a motive." I shrugged. "On the other hand, people have been murdered for far less. And he could have found out about her goings-on whenever he was gone."

"You don't suppose it really was a random killing, do you?"

I shook my head. "Both Mrs. Taylor and

Gray say she had a miserable head cold; she wouldn't have gone out and wasn't likely to let anyone visit either. At least not a male. She was too concerned with her looks. So how did she end up in the alley?''

''Maybe a woman? Certainly someone she knew. Had to be.''

''And they went for a stroll down the alley at that time of night? Come on, Martha. You can do better than that. And besides, she had a belly full of booze. Where did that come from? Everyone says she hardly drank at all.''

''Closet drinker?''

''I wonder if Sam will tell me what else is in Dr. Hazen's report.'' I reached for the phone. ''While I'm trying to get him, will you look up that art dealer we did the family tree for last year? I remembered him last night. I think his name was Perkins, Parsons, something like that.''

''Henry Porter. I'll get his number. For the La Tour thing?''

I nodded, dialing Sam's number. He picked up on the first ring, and was in a good mood, even after I asked about Dr. Hazen's report.

''Added some to what we already knew, but

not a lot," he said. "The primary cause of death was a form of alcohol poisoning. She died three to five minutes before her throat was cut. Which will probably complicate what he, or she, is charged with when we catch him. Hazen identified the stomach contents as almost eighty percent gin. He says it all went down at once and was probably forced down. He found bruising on the inside of her throat that might have been made by a tube, or something similar."

"Was there any other bruising? Hands? Wrists? I mean, how did anyone force it down her throat without tying her or holding her down?"

"No other bruising. She had probably passed out from the other stuff she'd been drinking. Her blood alcohol level was two point something."

"Whoa!"

"Yeah, loaded. And she was also loaded with enough antihistamines to make her groggy anyway."

"She had a bad cold. Both Mrs. Taylor and Steven Gray mentioned it when—"

"Confound it, Demary. What were you doing talking to Gray?'' Sam interrupted. ''How many times do I have to tell you—''

''Because I wanted to,'' I interrupted right back with a snap. ''At least we know he didn't kill her so he's a safe one to talk to. Be reasonable, will you? All I've been trying to do is get some kind of a picture of the woman in my mind.''

He made a harrumphing sound.

''And without much luck,'' I added.

''Who else have you talked to?'' he asked resignedly.

I gave him all I knew, without mentioning Joey or Sherry by name. He didn't need to know where I got my leads, and anyway, he probably guessed Joey put me on to Caro flooding Daniel's yard.

While I was telling him all, something we had been talking about in the last few minutes started tickling the back of my mind, but I couldn't put my finger on what it was.

Sam said something I missed and when I didn't answer he practically snarled at me.

''What? What?'' I asked.

''I asked if you wanted to go to dinner at the Topgallant tonight,'' he growled.

"The Topgallant? Whoops! What's the occasion? Not my birthday." The Topgallant is a very upscale restaurant on one of the top floors of the Columbia Tower, with elegant service, a spectacular view of the city, and marvelous food. Also pricey.

He hesitated. "Something I need to do there tonight," he said finally. "I want to be seated by seven-thirty, so I'll pick you up around six-thirty. Okay?"

I heard someone come into his office and say something to him and a moment later he told me he had to go, and hung up.

Just as he did I caught the elusive thought that had been niggling at me. I had assumed that Steven Gray was totally out of the picture as far as being a suspect, but that wasn't necessarily true. If I remembered correctly, he had been released from the San Francisco jail on Saturday afternoon but had waited for his two friends to be released before coming back on Monday. Why? And where had he been all that time? He had not gone back to his hotel. According to the coroner's report, Caro had died at approximately three o'clock Sunday morning. There was a lot of time between early Saturday afternoon and three o'clock Sunday morning.

And a lot of planes fly between Seattle and San Francisco.

NINETEEN

MARTHA CAME IN while Sam and I were talking and left a note on my desk with Henry Porter's number, so I called right away.

Mr. Porter himself answered and he remembered me. After a few minutes' chat about the job I'd done for him he asked, "What can I do for you, Miss Jones? Are you interested in buying an investment painting? Remember we talked about that once."

I laughed. "I wish I could say yes but I'm still not in that kind of financial position. No, what I wanted was to ask if you could give me any ideas on how to locate an art dealer named Benjamin Golder who was in business in Cologne in 1936. I've sent inquiries to the places I know of but thought you might know of somewhere else I could try." I told him what queries I'd already sent out.

"I think that about covers it as far as bureaucratic possibilities go," he said slowly. "But I do know of a man who might be able to help you on a personal level. His father owned an antique store in Cologne in that time period. Could you tell me why you need the information?"

I didn't see any reason not so I told him about the La Tour, without giving him any names.

"Could be worth a fortune if it's genuine," he said judiciously. "I presume your client is having it authenticated by an expert?"

"Yes, authenticating it isn't part of my brief. She wants me to make sure she isn't buying stolen property."

"Very commendable. Well, it's rather a long shot but William Sauer might be able to help you. I think William is in his eighties so I don't know how good his memory is anymore, but he might remember Golder's gallery, as many of the antique dealers and art galleries in Cologne used to be in the same district. He lives in London now. If you hold on for a moment I'll get his number for you."

Mr. Sauer's memory appeared to be in excellent condition. When I told him my problem and that I'd been given his name by Henry Porter he was quite willing to do his best for me, as he put it.

"The name Golder was so common then in Germany," he said regretfully. "It doesn't bring anyone specifically to mind. If you had the exact address that might be different."

"Oh, but I do," I told him. "In fact I have it right here." I scrabbled through the files on my desk, found the Hon. Violet's, and read off the address from Golder's letterhead.

"Hmm. Let me think a moment. No, that can't be correct. There's a memorial park, or square really, in that location now because that area was totally destroyed by the Allied bombing and I think, no, I'm positive, there were private homes and an apartment block there in the thirties. As I recall, the only shop was a small grocer and news agent. On the corner. Nothing in the way of a gallery. That street was quite beyond the gallery district."

"Did you live nearby?"

"Live, yes. Our house was nearby, but my father's antique shop was several blocks to the east in the center of the gallery district. However, we left Germany for England in the fall of 1934 so the area could have changed in the next few years. It's possible Mr. Golder's gallery replaced the grocers. I think it unlikely, but not impossible.''

''Why do you think it unlikely?''

''Life was beginning to be extremely troublesome for the Jewish community in Cologne by 1934-35 and it would have been very hard for a Jewish businessman to move into a new neighborhood. Do you understand?''

He obviously didn't want to elaborate so I told him I understood, thanked him for talking to me, and we hung up. When Hitler's party came into power in 1933 it immediately began to take systematic measures to eliminate Germany's Jewish population, but it did not get completely under way until 1938, following the death of a German diplomat by a Jewish assassin. After what was called Kristallnacht, the Night of Broken Glass.

So, although it may have been difficult for him, Mr. Golder could still have been doing business in 1936. I looked at the gallery receipt again, then put it back in the file. It certainly looked genuine. Mr. Sauer could be wrong; he could also be right. So far, there was no proof one way or the other that the shop, or Mr. Golder, had ever existed. I'd have to wait until I had answers from my other queries. But talking with Mr. Sauer had swung my thinking back a hundred and eighty degrees regarding Mr. Parrick and his La Tour painting. He seemed like such a nice guy, which should have told me something at the time. The first man who sold the Brooklyn Bridge was probably a nice guy too.

"Have you talked to Anna Carmine since she saw Roger, Caro's brother?" Martha asked, poking her head around the door.

"No. I forgot about his appointment. Why?"

"Anna's in her office and I think you ought to go talk to her. I'll tell you why when you come back."

I started to ask for an explanation but she turned and disappeared into the storeroom before I could say anything, so I went down to Anna's.

She greeted me with a smile and waved me to a chair. "What's on your mind, Demary?"

"Roger Crawford. Can you tell me what he wanted yesterday?"

"Sure. He isn't a client. Plus he acted so weird I'd like your slant on him."

I blinked, surprised. "Weird? Roger? I've only talked to him once but still…He sure didn't strike me as weird."

"Well, maybe that's the wrong word but from a legal standpoint he certainly struck me as weird. Personally he was charming, and full of small talk, but… He wanted to know who was responsible for Caro's remains."

"He *what?* How weird."

"So I said."

"But, I mean, why did he want to know? And if he was concerned, surely either Daniel or Steven Gray would be the ones to talk to. I know Steven wants to have her interred back East somewhere, where her parents are buried. He told me so. What did you tell him? Roger?"

"I told him I didn't have the faintest. To start with I wasn't her lawyer. Bigamy, if she did commit bigamy, isn't in my field of expertise but I do know that until that fact is established one way or the other, the question of her heir, or heirs, will hang in midair, as will who is legally responsible for her burial.

Unless she made out a will, of course, and she doesn't sound like the type to have done so.''

"I'll be darned. Did he say why he wanted to know?''

"He said if he was the one responsible he needed to make some arrangements, which sounded reasonable enough, but you're right, he should have been talking to Gray. Or Daniel for that matter. He didn't strike me as a stupid man and I couldn't figure why he thought he needed legal advice.''

"Did you charge him?''

"You bet I did! I'm not into freebies. I charged him for my time, not my advice. I didn't have any anyway. Something about him...I don't know. For all his looks and charm, I didn't like him.'' She stood up and stretched. Anna is tall and angular, a lot like Martha, and wears clothes beautifully too. Today she had on a tubelike garment in a turquoise blue with a string of faux pearls that hung to her hipbones.

Sometimes I feel like a midget surrounded by tall, beautiful models.

"As far as I know Caro didn't have anything to leave,'' I said. "And, anyway, wouldn't her interest in the house or her car or anything else like that go automatically to Steven?''

''Not necessarily. As I told Roger, the first thing that will have to be ascertained will be her legal marital status. Until that's established, what happens to anything is moot.''

''Have you heard from Daniel?'' I asked. ''I haven't.''

''Yes, as a matter of fact he called just before you came in.'' She grinned her gamine grin. ''I think the reason you haven't heard from him is because Martha intimidates him. She told him you did not like clients calling for reports, and anyway, you were out.''

''I was. And tell him not to let Martha buffalo him. She will if she can. She does everyone.''

After a while I wandered back to my own office. I started to tell Martha what Anna had said but she interrupted me before I could get started.

''I know all that; I talked to Anna earlier. I wanted you to hear it from her before I told you what I just learned.''

Martha's usually composed expression was

alive with something I couldn't quite define. Glee, maybe.

"Remember when we were talking motive and couldn't come up with one?" she asked.

"I remember, and I still can't."

"Well, how does somewhere in the neighborhood of a million dollars strike you?"

"Like a full load of cement."

"Remember my mate in Alameda, the one who faxed me the bumf on George Johnson? Caro and Roger's great-uncle?"

I nodded.

"Well, what she didn't tell me at the time, because she was just back from a long weekend in Acapulco with her husband and hadn't caught up with the news, was that George Johnson died last Friday. He left an estate of several million dollars and as he died before Caro did... Well, do you get the picture?"

"Wow! Do I! Caro's death means somebody around here stands to inherit one heck of a lot of money. Money—number one on the motive hit parade."

TWENTY

"THAT DOES OPEN an interesting can of worms, doesn't it?" I said thoughtfully.

Martha grinned. "Thought you'd like it. Gives you a whole new perspective. Are you going to tell that copper?"

I raised my eyebrows. "What copper?"

She went out snickering as my phone began to ring. She thinks Sam bosses me around too much. Which, coming from her, is really funny.

"Hi, Demary. What's going on?" Sherry asked when I answered. I'd left a "call me" message on her machine.

I started to laugh. "Just wait till I tell you," I said, between giggles. "It's not what I called you about, but hear this…." I gave her an abbreviated account of Martha's genealogy search.

"I don't believe it," Sherry said flatly. "Martha must have got it wrong. I can't possibly be related to that woman. She was wicked." Sherry has a very strict code of behavior.

"Now, now. Let's not be speaking ill of the dead," I said in my most sanctimonious tone. "And besides that, Martha doesn't make mistakes."

"Well, she better not tell anyone or I'll throttle her, I will." She began to laugh. "Of all the crazy things. Wait till I tell my mother."

"Gee. I wouldn't if I were you. She'll have a hissy fit." Sherry's mother was a charter member of the prim and proper club and she definitely wouldn't like the idea of being related, however distantly, to a murder victim. She had a hard enough time dealing with her daughter being a model.

"You got a point there," Sherry agreed. "Well, if this wasn't what you were waiting to spring on me, what was it?"

"How did the shoot go?" I asked. I wasn't sure now that I wanted to ask her about Scott. Sherry was such a guileless creature she was sure to say something that would alert him.

"Awful. Perfectly awful. Talk about a nightmare trip. Scott picked me up. He has a new

car and he was so darn fussy about parking it
we nearly missed the plane to start with. Then
our connection in New York was messed up
somehow and we didn't get into Reykjavik until three in the morning and had be ready to
shoot by eight because of the light. The boots
that went with the outfit were a size too small
and I had to stand for hours in the blasted
things and...Well, anyway, it was simply
dreadful.''

"That must have been miserable," I said,
not feeling too awfully sorry for her. Tight
boots were a small price to pay for the fees she
got. I decided against saying anything about
Scott and instead asked her to come have lunch
with me at Julia's on Forty-fourth and Wallingford.

She agreed, and forty-five minutes later I
was ordering my favorite, pasta Marisole, an
absolutely fabulous fettucine dish with arti-
choke hearts, sun-dried tomatoes, mushrooms,
and pine nuts. Sherry ordered the same.

While we were waiting to be served I got
Sherry talking about going through Customs in
the different countries. As I suspected, a group
such as hers was rarely stopped at all and when

they were it was only to ask how long they were going to be there. As both Scott and his assistant always carried their cameras and equipment with them, understandably not wanting to take a chance on their baggage getting lost, it was obvious what they were in the country for. Plus the fact that Sherry, like any other famous model, was easily recognized.

"Do you know Scott's grandfather, Mr. Parrick?" I asked casually as the waitress set our salad in front of us.

"Uh-huh. Nice old guy. He does the most beautiful paintings. They're all over the house. Why? Do you know him?"

"Not really. He's selling a La Tour that belonged to his grandfather to one of my clients, so I was out to his place talking to him about it the other day."

"Oh, I didn't realize he ever— Oh, thanks." Sherry moved her salad as the waitress brought our pasta. She dug in immediately. "I'm starved. Among other things, I didn't have a decent meal the whole time I was gone. The hotel there has wonderful food but with one thing and another we just never had a chance to eat anything except a packed lunch. And you know me. I like my food."

I grinned. Sherry did indeed like to eat well. How she maintained her pencil-thin figure was a mystery.

"While we're on the subject of people, relatives that is, how about a George Johnson? Lives in Alameda?" I asked. I hadn't mentioned him when I was giving her the genealogy rundown.

"If he's the same one I'm thinking of I don't know him, but I know who he is. He's some kind of a distant relative of my mother's."

I all but choked on a mouthful of my pasta. "You've heard about him?" I gasped.

She gave me a surprised look. "As I said, I know who he is. Aunt Edna is into keeping in touch. She has a whole list of relatives she sends her horrid annual Christmas letter to and is always trying to get Mom to do the same. What's got you all excited about him?"

"Did you know he was a millionaire? And that he died recently?"

"No! Really? Be nice if he left Mom something, but I doubt it. When I said distant I did mean distant. He's some kind of a sixteenth cousin or something. Mom has never had any contact with him.''

''I wouldn't be too sure about that.'' I went on to tell her about his will.

She shrugged. ''If Martha's friend has it right, and being a newspaper reporter she likely has it completely backward, it still doesn't mean my mother will inherit anything significant. A million doesn't go all that far when you split it up among a couple of dozen or more people. And particularly not when you're talking a third of the total. Who will inherit Caro's share? Do you know yet?''

''No, and if Anna's right it will be a while before anybody knows.'' Between mouthfuls of pasta I gave her an abbreviated account of Caro's marital status.

''Somehow that sounds like her,'' Sherry said, making a little moue of distaste. ''When I was getting my hair done Monday one of the girls told me Caro was forever not showing up for an appointment, or being an hour late, and then telling Raphael that he had the time wrong.'' She stared off into space for a moment. ''You know, when I stop to think about it, Caro really wasn't a very nice person.''

I laughed. "No kidding." Sherry has absolutely no sense of humor.

"No, I mean it," she said seriously. "I think she had a vindictive streak too."

That was new. "What makes you say that?"

"She got one of the exercise girls at the club fired because she overheard her talking about her and Don Ward. And it wasn't just that she got her fired, it was the way she did it. She accused the girl of stealing. Everyone knew it was just because the poor girl had been talking about her. Don's sister, Sara Lee, said it was just one more example of what a rotten person Caro was. But let's talk about something else, shall we? I'm beginning to really dislike even thinking about her. I'm sorry about what happened to her but I still can't like her."

I agreed.

After we finished our lunch we went over to the Interlake Mall and wandered around for a bit, so I didn't get back to the office until three. I told Martha to keep everyone away from me for a few minutes, and sat down to think. Talking to Sherry had made me realize I was wrong about one thing. Caro's killer might not have had a big honking motive. A lot of people disliked her in varying degrees, and as unlikely as it felt to me, one of them might have just disliked her enough to kill her.

The motive could be something as small as getting fired unfairly—although getting fired may not have been small for the exercise girl—or as big as a sister committing suicide, or Caro's share of George Johnson's estate. Or— The thought jumped into my mind like a ten-pound barbell. Caro might have been heavily insured. Gray worked for an insurance company. What could be more natural than for him to take out a big policy on her? Most such companies routinely insured their employees and their families anyway.

He had the time, he could have found out what she got up to when he was gone, and money was always a prime mover. The combination of money—insurance money—and her perfidious behavior added up to one strong motive. George Johnson's estate may not have entered into the equation at all. I needed to take a harder look at Steven Gray.

TWENTY-ONE

I DECIDED ON the direct approach and called Gray at his office—a thoroughly unprofessional thing to do. He had every right to be furious and hang up on me but surprisingly he didn't.

"I wondered when someone would think of the insurance," he said, sounding amused. "And if I didn't have a very solid alibi for the time involved I might have been worried. However, yes, I did have Caro insured for a sizable amount, a regular company practice. And I am the beneficiary. But, as I say, I do have a solid alibi. I was in jail."

He sounded so smug I wanted to tell him flying time between Seattle and San Francisco was only about three hours. He had not been in jail the entire weekend and he'd had plenty of time to come home and cut Caro's throat before he met his friends on Monday morning.

But I didn't. I made my excuses, thanked

him prettily, and rang off. I had a hard time learning it, but sometimes it is smarter to keep your mouth shut.

THAT EVENING, getting ready for my date with Sam, I discovered my new citron-colored silk dress had shrunk. It hadn't been off its padded hanger since I bought it but it was certainly snugger than when I'd tried it on two weeks ago.

I thought about the pasta I'd had for lunch and made another mental note to get to my aerobics class in the morning, ran a comb through my hair, and was ready when Sam rang the doorbell. He looked great in dark blue seersucker slacks and a blue tweed jacket. Sam has always been a darn good-looking guy, kind of a combination Robert Redford/Paul Newman, only with dark hair and dimples, and he gets better looking all the time. Which irritates me no end. It's so unfair. Men age—like fine wine, women get old, and there is a whole world of difference between the two words.

I never could get Sam to tell me why he wanted to be at the Topgallant that night but it was a successful evening from the very beginning anyway. The first person I saw when we were escorted to our table was Steven Gray just three tables away with a rather plain but charming-appearing woman who I knew instinctively was his ex-wife Nancy. I thought at first they might be the reason Sam was there but he took a chair facing the other way and didn't pay any attention to them, although I know he saw them. He has a way of giving any room he enters a sweeping once-over that takes in just about everything.

Steven was being very attentive to Nancy and I wondered if I was seeing a reconciliation in progress. It became more than speculation when he saluted her with his glass of wine and then leaned over to kiss her. A rather lengthy kiss, too, for the middle of a public dining room.

Sometime during the entrée, pan-fried Olympia oysters in my case, Sam's attitude changed from tense and watchful to simply enjoying himself. Unfortunately I hadn't been paying close enough attention to him so I never caught a glimpse of what he was there for. I was too busy watching Gray and Nancy, wondering

what their getting together signified, if anything.

Sam was in such a fun mood from then on
that I invited him in for dessert when he
brought me back to my door. As a result I
didn't get to sleep until late, very late. Sam can
be terrific company at times. I like to choose
the times though.

THE FIRST THING I did when I got to the office
Friday morning was have Martha get a fax
copy of Steven Gray's first marriage license,
and sure enough, Nancy had been born in San
Francisco. And I'd bet my bottom dollar her
parents still lived there. A quick long-distance
call proved me right. Steven Gray may or may
not have known what Caro was up to and may
or may not have been planning to divorce her,
but I felt almost certain he'd been visiting his
ex-wife's parents Saturday night. That was his
real alibi, not being in jail.

Martha didn't think much of ex-in-laws as
an alibi. ''It would be the same as a wife ali-
biing a husband. The DA would have to be daft
to believe it,'' she said, shaking her head. ''I
still think Steven could have found out about

Caro and gone spare. Hired a hit man. Especially if he had in mind to go back to wife number one.''

"But why bother? If the marriage was bigamous all he had to do was walk out. Or tell her to leave."

"But he didn't think it was. Or at least that's what he told you."

I snorted. "And he'd certainly tell me the truth! Yeah, right!''

I was convinced Sam knew Steven's real San Francisco alibi and hadn't told me out of sheer orneriness. Which, in retrospect, made me good and mad. I should have kicked him off my front step, not invited him in. In fact, the more I thought about it the madder I got. By the time Carol Ann called a half hour later I was so teed off at him I agreed immediately when she asked if I wanted to go to Ocean Shores for the weekend with her, her longtime boyfriend, Frank Kettle, and Jake Allenby.

"Frank made a three-bedroom suite reservation," she said, naming the resort hotel. "All the rooms have two double beds, plus all the couches make up into beds. There will be plenty of room and it won't cost much if we share. Ruth and Helen, from records, are coming and probably Helen's brother with his two kids. This great weather isn't going to last much longer. Come play in the sun while it's still here.''

As good an excuse as I needed.

"Sounds like fun," I agreed. "I may be late getting away from here so I'll take my own car. I should be there by nine though.'' She said that was okay and rang off. Taking my own car would give me a chance to check up on Roger Crawford's alibi. The place he'd stayed that weekend was a few miles farther up the coast in another small resort town called Moclips.

Sam would be wild when he found out where I'd gone, and who else was going, and I knew I could trust Carol Ann to see that he did hear. Which would serve him right, besides making him look foolish if I found a hole in Roger's alibi that he'd missed.

In the first place Sam had no right to be jealous; Jake and I were simply good friends. And if we were ever more than that, it was none of Sam's business.

With that thought in mind, I went back to work feeling thoroughly pleased with life.

The Hon. Violet called a few minutes later, sending my good mood right down the drain. I had told her, as I told every client, that I would send her a written account of what I'd done, or not done, at the end of the week or when I had something positive to report, whichever came sooner. I do not like clients calling me. Not only does it interrupt whatever I'm doing at the time, it bugs me.

Her interpretation of "the end of the week" was on Friday, not a week from the day she'd hired me.

"Ridiculous," she said tartly when I explained. "Friday is the end of the week. Now, what have you accomplished?"

I was very tempted to say Not a darn thing, but I controlled myself. "I do not have anything positive," I said coolly. "In fact, what I do have so far is negative. The only German authority that has had time to respond to my query has no record of the gallery, as such, paying taxes in the year the painting was supposedly purchased. That does not mean the gallery wasn't there. Times were getting very chaotic in Germany. Mr. Golder may have been doing business out of his home, may have left

Germany, may simply have chosen not to pay his taxes, or may have paid under a different name. Or he might have been in Buchenwald by that time. At this point I don't know.''

''Very trying.''

''Yes, I believe it was a trying time,'' I said smoothly. ''Particularly for anyone with that name.''

Dead silence for thirty seconds. ''I'll be expecting your report,'' she said, and broke the connection.

That tickled me. I wouldn't have thought retreat was in the Hon. Violet's line.

TWENTY-TWO

I HAD NO SOONER put the phone down than the thing rang again. This time it was Daniel.

"Well, it's about time I heard from you," I said.

"Can I take that as an overwhelming desire for my company?" he asked.

"Nope, sorry. But I did want to talk to you. I'd like the name of your hostess Saturday night."

"You're checking my alibi?" he asked, his tone suddenly flat, almost annoyed.

"No," I said, surprised, reminding me again that I didn't really know Daniel very well. "At least, not in the sense you mean, but I would like a closer idea of when you got home. You must have come home before Caro, uh, died or you would have run over her. I am checking an alibi but it doesn't happen to be yours."

"Oh. Uh, seems ridiculous," he said after a

pause. "But no one, including myself, has a clear idea of when I left that blasted party. It was quite a while after one o'clock; I know that because we had pizza delivered at twelve-forty-five. Or at least so the pizza delivery boy says. There were seventeen people there and of course we were all milling around, eating pizza, drinking beer, talking. It wasn't a heavy drinking party so no one was drunk or anything like that, but it's an old three-story house with a recreation room in the basement so we were scattered on two floors. I thought I must have left before two but one of the women said she was keeping an eye on the time because she promised her baby-sitter to be back by two-thirty and I was definitely still there when she and her husband left."

"So, say you left at two-thirty. How long would it take you to get home?"

"At that time of night about twenty minutes. The house is in Ballard."

That meant Caro was not on the garage floor before three o'clock. If he was right about when he left. "Does, uh, Lieutenant Morgan know this?"

"Yes. He talked to several people at the party."

I cussed to myself. Why in the world was Sam being so perverse? He couldn't be jealous of Daniel too, could he?

After we hung up I thought of another question I should have asked him. Most government employees have automatic insurance for themselves and their families, both health and life, and I wondered if he had ever collected on Caro's insurance. Supposing that he had any. I didn't believe he'd had anything to do with her death, but if he'd collected on her insurance, it would give him a whale of a motive because he would have to repay it. Or would he? She was certainly dead enough now.

Later, when Martha came in with a fax that had just come in from Germany, I was still mentally wrestling with alibis. None were what I'd call really solid. As far as the time frame went neither Daniel nor Steven Gray were totally out of the picture as villains, nor was Caro's brother, Roger. And I needed to find out who Caro's unknown friends were, the ones who brought her home in the middle of the night via the alley. Anyone of them could be guilty, although as she seemed to have been playing the field, so to speak, it didn't sound as if any of them could be close enough to generate the passion needed to commit murder.

The fax was from an art historian I'd written to in Munich. He could find no trace of Benjamin Golder or his gallery but thought that not unusual as his own interest was more concerned with the art works themselves rather than their provenance. He said the painting could possibly be genuine as it was well known that La Tour painted several on the subject, but he personally doubted it and recommended that Mrs. Barcasie have it authenticated by at least two experts. None of which got me any forwarder.

"I've also got the lowdown on Roger's finances," Martha said when I looked up from the fax. I'd told her to see what she could find out about his financial status.

"Already?

"Easy. Dead easy, in fact. I called that real estate gal we did the skip-trace for. She didn't know Roger herself but she knew someone who did. No proof of course, but as far as is generally known Roger is in good shape. No

multimillionaire by any means but certainly
comfortable. Most of his money is tied up in
property and Bellevue is a prosperous community so, according to her, he should be okay
for the foreseeable future. It's all hearsay
though, so if you want anything more solid it
will take a little time.''

"Doesn't give him much of a motive, does
it? Unless there's something besides Uncle
George's money involved. I'm still going to
check out his alibi though; that visit to Anna
was peculiar.''

"What's to check? He was in Ocean Shores,
wasn't he?''

"Actually, he wasn't. He was at a small motel in Moclips, up the coast from Ocean Shores.
But that isn't the point. He left there at eight
Sunday morning and took the leisurely way
home. He stopped at a restaurant in Aberdeen
for breakfast, wandered around the countryside
some, and had lunch at Hawk's Prairie Restaurant in Olympia. A busboy there, a sharp kid
named Paul, remembers him distinctly. He got
home late in the afternoon. All clear as moun-
tain dew. But Caro was already dead by the
time he left Moclips. What he doesn't have is

an alibi for Saturday night. Nobody at the motel
saw him after four in the afternoon. Which
leaves him sixteen hours unaccounted for.''

''What does he say?''

''According to Carol Ann he says he went
beach-combing, had dinner at a small café, had
a beer in a tavern, and went to bed. He doesn't
remember any times.''

''Did they check with the local taverns?''

''Yes, but Carol Ann says the checker was
a local cop and she doubts that he did more
than talk to the one closest to the motel. They
saw him several times in the three days he was
there but can't specifically remember him on
Saturday night. Said they were too busy to remember who was in the place. The waitress
might remember but she went on vacation Sunday so talking to her will have to wait until she
gets back sometime next week. Which reminds
me, see if the gal in Bellevue can fax us a
picture of Roger. He's a prominent businessman; there should have been a picture of him
in the local paper at one time or an other. I
want to take one with me if I can.''

"Take it where? To Ocean Shores? When are you going?"

"This evening."

She nodded and went out.

I spent the next hour updating my file on Caro, answering a couple of e-mail queries I'd sent out regarding my research for Mrs. Dobbe in Astoria, and framing another letter to the Cologne equivalent of our County/City Building. Power department records probably wouldn't go back to the 1930s, as they were frequently private enterprise, but water department records might. They were usually city government. Or at least they were in this country. It was worth a shot anyway and a query to them could be faxed.

Joey was coming up the street toward the office when I went out at eleven to go to the QFC for a container of peach Yoplait.

"Taking my mother to a funeral," he said quickly when I couldn't hide my surprise at the suit and tie he was wearing. He looked like a different young man. Older, and very classy.

"Oh, dear. I hope not someone close," I said, prepared to be sympathetic.

"Nope, guy she went to school with. But she

doesn't want to go alone. You know if the cops have talked to the people in the house across from the dead one?"

"No, I don't know for sure, but they usually do talk to the people on both sides of the street. Why?"

"Lady straight across from the Grays' has a new baby. New babies mostly wake up all night long. I know. We got one next door. Doesn't make any difference what time you look out the window, the light is on in that baby's room and you can see the dad walking the kid back and forth. Don't know how the poor guy ever gets to work in the morning. Probably the only place he gets any rest, though. You go talk to new mom across from the Grays'. Don't think she'd talk to me. She's just staying there with her folks for a while and don't know me."

"Hm-m-m. What makes you think—"

"Go try," he said sternly. "She's using the front upstairs bedroom, looks right out at the Grays' place. People there is named White. I don't know the new momma's last name but her first name is Jenny."

He glanced at his watch, something else I'd

never seen him wear before, and told me he
had to go. "You be sure now," he said and off
he went.

I nodded meekly, wondering where he got
all his information. Joey is very seldom wrong,
however, and he was so emphatic I decided to
skip the Yoplait and check the house out right
away, see if the upstairs bedroom did have a
good view across the street. Mrs. Taylor had
mentioned Mrs. White too, indicating that she
could see what went on around the Gray place.
With Mrs. Taylor's name as an entrée they
might tell me more than they would, the police.
It certainly wouldn't hurt to try. And it would
please Joey.

I was in luck, and glad I went when I did.
When I pulled up in front of the Whites' house
a few minutes later a young woman with a
baby in her arms was standing on the sidewalk
talking to Mrs. Taylor. Mrs. Taylor recognized
me immediately and motioned me out of the
car.

"I'm so pleased you came along," she said
after introducing me to the young mother.
"Jenny here has something interesting to tell
you. I think she may have seen Caro's murderer."

TWENTY-THREE

JOEY, AS USUAL, had been absolutely right. The new baby had been keeping his mother awake. She had been rocking him in a chair by the window, and had seen Caro come home at three-fifteen in the morning. She was positive about the time.

"Did you see her clearly enough to recognize her?" I asked. "I mean, as opposed to simply seeing a woman's figure."

"Oh yes, it was Caro all right, and Caro's car, although she wasn't driving." She nodded across the street. "See the big light above their garage door? It's one of those kind that go on automatically as soon as it gets dark and it lights up the whole yard." She grinned. "It's no wonder she had her boyfriends bring her home by the alley. The front is lit up like a carnival at night. There's another big light on the porch."

"How about the driver? Was it a man?"

She nodded.

"Did you recognize him? Or would you know him if you saw him again?"

She thought a moment. "No, I don't think I could pick him out of a lineup or anything, like in the movies, but I do know it wasn't Mr. Gray. I've known him for years and it wasn't him. I saw his face when he helped her out of the car; he had to practically lift her out and he was facing toward me, but it was just a man's face."

"Dark hair? Light? Was he tall, short? Anything at all that you can remember. Shut your eyes and try to see him in your mind. Sometimes that helps."

She closed her eyes obediently. The baby made little mewing sounds. She patted it absently and after a pause said, "He got out of the car and went around the hood to open the door on her side. Funny he should do that. You would have thought he'd go around the back. The hood was only a couple of feet from the garage door. He had to go sideways. He must have been trying to stay out of sight." She stopped and thought. "He was trying not to make any noise too. He could have just slammed the car door with his foot, but he held her out of the way and shut it quiet.''

"Did you have the light on in your room?"

Her eyes popped open. "No, I should say not. I never would have got Brian here back to sleep if the light had been on.'' She shut her eyes again. "He opened the door on Caro's side and got her out of the car. I think she was drunk; he had a time getting her out. He had dark hair and I think it was curly.'' She paused, thinking. "He was medium size but he was strong. At one point he was almost holding her off the ground and he was doing it with one arm while he shut the car door.''

"Are you sure about his hair?"

"Yes. It was dark and curly."

"Did he carry her then?"

"Oh no. She walked around the back with him. He was holding her up but she was alive.''

Her tone was so casual it made me faintly sick. Young people her age had been born into such a violent world, both in reality and on the screen, they seemed to take a brutal death as a matter of course. The attitude frightened me.

Mrs. Taylor told me later that Jenny was just eighteen.

I asked if she'd told the police.

"No, I wasn't here when they came, I was at the doctor's, and my mother never thought to tell them that I was staying. Johnny, my husband, works shares on a fish boat. He's in Alaska. He won't be back for another six weeks and I didn't want to stay in the apartment alone while the baby was so little. I'll be going back to my own place in a week or so though."

"I think you'd better call Lieutenant Morgan and tell him," I said reluctantly. "It might be important to know exactly when she got home."

She shrugged. "All right, I'll call him but I'm not going downtown. He'll have to come out here. I don't like taking Brian out where there are a lot of people around. He isn't two weeks old yet."

Mrs. Taylor caught the expression on my face and interpreted it correctly, nodding slightly as if in agreement. Young Brian had been less than a week old when his momma sat rocking him in the night, watching a killer lead his victim to her death. The tiny boy had *certainly* been born into a violent world.

"THAT LEAVES STEVEN OUT," I told Martha after reporting my conversation with young Jenny and Mrs. Taylor.

"I guess," she said reluctantly. "Unless, as I said before, he hired someone. But I have to admit I'm beginning to doubt he did."

I nodded. "The man who brought her home was too careless to be a hired hand. He parked in the front drive, in full view, and then walked her down the alley to Daniel's garage. Why? It wasn't standing open. Daniel distinctly remembers closing it. Did her killer know it was Daniel's garage? Did he know Caro had been, or still was, married to him? Was he deliberately trying to implicate Daniel?"

Martha stared at me for a moment and then said, "If you're asking me, yes. I think he was trying to implicate Daniel. There was simply no other reason for leaving her body where he did."

"And the dark hair leaves Daniel out."

"Unless he was wearing a wig," she said with a sour smile. She didn't think Daniel was guilty any more than I did.

"And another thing," I said, ignoring her. "Why did he leave her car in the drive? Why didn't he use the electronic door opener and go inside where no one could have seen him? Why were they in her car to start with? And how did he get home?"

"Get home? What difference does it make? Maybe he walked. Maybe his car was parked nearby. Maybe he called a cab." She stopped, thought a moment. "You know, that may be worth calling the cab companies about. He could have walked over to the U district and called a cab from there. Maybe from the lobby of the Meany Hotel. It's open all night."

"That's a thought, but no, there's something wrong with the entire scenario. And especially that night. She had a bad cold; she wouldn't have wanted to go out at all. And certainly not with any of her boyfriends. Plus she was in her own car which wasn't the norm when she was meeting any of them. No, I don't think the man Jenny saw was a friend of any kind."

"You're not back to the wandering homicidal maniac, are you?"

I scowled at her. "Driving her car? Don't be silly."

"Who then? Her brother?"

"Possibly." I swore to myself. "I just don't know. There's something out of kilter with the timing and everything else. None of it hangs together. The alibis are too pat and at the same time none of them are really solid. Nobody has a clear motive either. And other than the boy-friends, there aren't any other suspects. I'm going to have to rethink the whole thing. I'm missing something somewhere."

"Well, the best of British luck to you. I'm leaving," she said, getting up. "I told Charles I'd be home early. Captain Tyson has invited us to dinner."

"Aboard the *Shady Lady?*" I asked in considerable surprise, wondering what had persuaded her to agree. Not that Captain Tyson's sailboat, the *Shady Lady,* wasn't a trim little craft. Although I personally doubted that it was seaworthy. Martha disliked boats of any kind. Like Sam, she could get seasick without ever leaving the dock.

"Don't be daft. We're going to the Salmon House. And be sure you lock up the front when

you leave. Anna is already gone for the weekend and so is Harry. In fact I think we're the
last ones here.''

She gave me a brief wave and went out, but
was back a moment later to hand me several
pictures.

"I nearly forgot these. They came while you
were gone. They're all of Roger Crawford.
Joan Farmer, the real estate gal in Bellevue,
sent them. Roger is active in the Chamber of
Commerce over there and has had his picture
in a half dozen things. She faxed the lot. Have
fun.''

She left again.

The pictures were all in color and one in
particular was very good. It was a cover shot
for a real estate brochure.

I worked a while longer keyboarding in my
conversation with young Jenny and Mrs. Taylor and then quit for the day too. It was almost
five by that time and Ocean Shores was a good
four hours away. I needed to pack, eat something, and fill up with gas. Running on empty
didn't cut it on the freeway.

TWENTY-FOUR

MY PACKING CONSISTED OF throwing a jacket, an extra pair of jeans, T-shirts, and some sweats into an old airline bag along with a few things like toothpaste and a hairbrush. It was still unseasonably warm in Seattle but I knew it would be cooler on the ocean. At the last minute I added a pair of cream-colored Dockers and a silk shirt in case we ate in the hotel dining room Saturday night, but I doubted that I'd use them. We're more a burger and french fry crowd.

For once the traffic on Interstate 5 wasn't bumper to bumper and was moving along at a reasonable rate of speed. I made the turn at Olympia onto Highway 8, was rolling through Aberdeen a little after eight o'clock and into Ocean Shores at nine.

The whole gang was there by that time, including Helen's widowed brother, James, with his two-year-old twins, Brendan and Colleen.

Helen and James and Carol Ann were trying to put the twins to bed when I got there. It takes three lively adults sometimes. I got to give them a good-night hug before they were finally tucked in. They are about the cutest pair I've ever seen and so funny. Brendan, the tallest by about a half inch, is as sturdy as a Seahawk linebacker, and has a sweet, placid makeup. Colleen on the other hand is a dainty little elfinlike creature with dimples, long golden hair, and the disposition of an agitated hamster. She thinks nothing of whacking her brother with anything handy when he does something that displeases her. Brendan never seems to mind but he does occasionally give her a good solid push onto her little fanny.

Somebody had brought a huge bowl of fresh-cooked, unshelled shrimp and after the twins were taken care of we all sat around until after midnight, eating shrimp, drinking—mostly soda pop—and talking. Subjects ran the gamut, from the possibility of the Seahawks signing a new quarterback to the latest scandal that was titillating the local Seattle scene. The so-called scandal was hilarious, or at least we thought so. It involved three well-known sisters of ad-

vanced years—I think the youngest claimed to
be ninety-four—a much younger gentleman of
eighty-seven and, of all things, an elderly Pe-
kingese all three ladies claimed to be an en-
gagement gift from the gentleman in question.
Charges of theft, dognapping, burglary, and un-
due influence were being flung in all directions,
and gleefully reported on the local news.

We didn't talk shop that evening but over
coffee the next morning Carol Ann told me the
San Francisco P.D. had interviewed Gray's ex-
in-laws. Despite disliking Steven because of the
divorce they had to admit that he had been with
them until late Sunday morning. An airtight alibi.

"So where does that leave you?" Carol Ann
asked. She wasn't working the case and didn't
know a whole lot more than I did.

"If Roger's alibi holds water, I'm up that
famous creek," I admitted. "Jenny, the new
little mother across the street from the Grays'
house, is positive Caro was alive at three-
fifteen. Daniel was home by then. He could
have killed her."

"But you don't think so."

I shook my head no. I didn't want to think so.

"You should be more choosy about your boyfriend," Carol Ann said, leering at me. She has a primitive sense of humor.

Later that afternoon I drove on up the highway to Moclips where I spent a little time driving around the few streets that made up the town to familiarize myself with where different places were in relation to the motel where Roger had stayed. Neither the town nor the motel were what I'd have thought Roger would choose. The motel in particular was small and shabby and offered nothing but its proximity to the beach. I flashed the woman in the office there my identification, handed her Roger's picture, and asked if she remembered him.

A tall, thin woman with a chilly manner, she wore a plastic name tag that identified her as Clara Sanders. She took Roger's picture from me, gave it a brief glance, and handed it back.

"I'm trying to establish exactly where Mr. Crawford went after he left the office here," I told her, trying to sound as if I had a right to expect an answer.

She remembered him all right—his looks are

pretty unforgettable—but she wasn't pleased with the memory, nor with me. "So somebody hired you to come down here and ask more questions," she said, giving me a sour look. "Well, I can't tell you anymore than I've already told the police. He came in the office about four o'clock Saturday and said he wanted to settle up his bill as he might leave early. I ran his Visa card, he signed it, and he left. He said he was going to go down to the beach but whether he did or not I don't know. And beyond that I can't tell you a thing."

"But you did see him again Sunday morning?"

"I saw his car. Driving out of the lot. It was five minutes after eight o'clock."

"He did go down to the beach," the teenage girl sorting registration slips at the far end of the counter spoke up. She looked and sounded like a younger version of Clara. A much pleasanter version.

"How do you know?" Clara snapped. "You were vacuuming seventeen and nineteen. You can't see the beach from this side of the building."

"I was putting the vacuum away in the storeroom. And straightening the blankets and sheets. Someone had them all messed about.'' She gave what I guessed now was her older sister a sly smile. ''You can see the beach trail from in there.''

''Could you tell what direction he took?'' I asked, trying to short-circuit the sibling antagonism, or whatever it was.

She turned her attention to me. ''North. Up toward the reservation. But he couldn't have gone far. It gets too rough up past the creek. Anyway, it's posted. You aren't supposed to be on reservation land without permission.''

''Oh, for heaven's sake, Becky,'' Clara snapped. ''The reservation is miles. He wouldn't have gone that far.''

''That's what I said,'' Becky said, smug. She turned back to her registration cards and I started to leave but had another thought as I opened the door.

''Where did he have his car parked?'' I asked Clara. ''Here by the office? Or in the lot on the other side of the building?''

''Neither one. Not on Saturday anyway. Young Andy had it up to his dad's garage to change the oil.''

"When did he bring it back?"

She shrugged. "I have no idea."

I nodded and went on out, making a mental note to talk to young Andy. But first I was going to go follow in Roger's footsteps. Not that I expected to find any sign of his passing; I just wanted to see what Roger had seen as he walked along the beach.

The path through the dunes wandered back and forth around piles of debris left by winter storms. I could hear the dull roar of the surf but I couldn't see the ocean until I topped the last sandy rise and it was spread out in front of me, an endless, moving sheet of water fading into the distant skyline. A gentle incoming tide splashed against the rocks, bits of bark swirling through the water like confetti. Countless tiny shore birds raced the bubbling wave scallops up the beach, then swept into flight in an unbelievable display of coordinated movement, an air-spun ballet that had me rooted in place until they disappeared into the distance.

I turned away, finally, and trudged north through the soft sand above the waterline. For a while the tops of buildings were visible above the dunes on the landward side but soon they were farther apart and then there was nothing but the sand and the sea.

I stopped after a while and sat on a log, not thinking, just enjoying the peace and solitude. The space, the immeasurable expanse of water, the constant waves swirling across the sand all mesmerized me, and, for a while at least, I forgot all my niggling little problems.

I had gone about two miles and was about to turn back—walking in soft sand is hard work—when I saw another path through the dunes. It was the first one I'd seen since the buildings had disappeared from sight. I followed it back toward the highway; I knew it paralleled the shoreline. I tramped through a belt of jack pines, and finally emerged onto a graveled parking lot with an old café and tavern on one side and a garage on the other.

I wasn't surprised when the teenager polishing an ancient Chevy Impala parked by the side of the garage turned out to be Andy, nor when he agreed he'd changed the oil in Roger's Saab on Saturday afternoon.

"Good-lookin' car, that Saab is," he remarked judiciously. "Not got the power this baby has though.'' He patted the Impala's flank.

"When did he pick it up?'' I asked. "Or did you take it back to the motel?''

"I took him and the car back to the motel after Pa closed up,'' he said, nodding toward the tavern. "He weren't that bad off but Pa didn't want him driving. Saturday night, always a bunch a drunks on the road. Nothing much else to do around here Saturday night 'cept get drunk or get in a fight.'' He shrugged. "That's the way it is in a small town. You have to allow for it.''

A teenage philosopher. With an ironclad alibi for Roger.

TWENTY-FIVE

I DROVE TO WORK Tuesday morning, going out of my way a few blocks to stop at the new little bagel shop down near the freeway for one of their fresh bagels with pimento cream cheese. Not that I needed any extra calories. Everything I owned seemed to have shrunk lately.

The cream-cheese bagel was my last indulgence for a while. As soon as I checked in with Martha I was on my way out to the Cascade View Health Club. Sherry was meeting me there at nine-thirty for a workout that she claimed was guaranteed to take at least an inch off any unwanted bulges.

Truth to tell, I wasn't all that worried about bulges—I'd just wear sweats and quit looking in the mirror for a while. Like Scarlett, I'd worry about that tomorrow. What I did want to do was to pump Sherry for information without her realizing I was doing so. Not a nice thing to do to a friend but it was for her own sake. She was due to go on a ten-day photo shoot in Rome with Scott before too long and I didn't want her inadvertently alerting him to the digging I was doing into his past, and his present. I had received a whole batch of replies Monday to my queries about the La Tour, all of them pointing to the possibility, actually probability, of the picture being a fraud. Sherry's remark about Adam Parrick's painting ability had gone right over my head at the time she made it, when we were eating lunch at Julia's, but I did remember later, and the combination gave me the first glimmerings of an idea.

One of my replies from Germany had stated unequivocally that there had never been a gallery at that address. The premises had been occupied continuously by members of the same family from 1898 to late 1943 when the house had been destroyed by Allied bombing. Of course that did not mean that the painting wasn't a genuine La Tour, but it certainly threw considerable doubt on its provenance.

As Mr. Sauer said, when I called him again in England, conditions in Germany were so hectic by 1936 there could be any number of

explanations for Benjamin Golder's use of a
fake address, or, and I hadn't thought of this
before, he could have lived in the house. I'd
have to check on that. Considering all the other
aspects of the case though, I couldn't think of
an explanation I'd believe in and, anyway, I
needed something more solid than my gut feeling before I told the Hon. Violet she'd been
had. And for that, I needed more information
about Scott. Martha had fobbed Violet off with
one of those "in the mail" stories when she'd
called bright and early Monday morning for a
report, but I couldn't do that again.

A few minutes later I zipped back down
Forty-fifth to Montlake and wound my way
through the Arboretum and down Madison to
the club. Sherry wasn't there but had left a
message for me with Connie, the receptionist.

"She said to tell you she had to go in to the
studio for some extra shots and wouldn't be
able to get here much before noon," Connie
told me. "She signed you in as her guest
though, so you can either go ahead and work
out now, or come back later. Whatever you
want."

I started to say I'd be back but changed my

mind and said I'd at least do sometime on the treadmill. I'd caught a glimpse of Sara Lee in a bright orange spandex workout suit going into the exercise room and I'd been wanting to talk to her.

She was on one of the StairMasters when I got changed and joined her. She didn't look too pleased to see me but she grunted a greeting so I decided her expression had more to do with the effort she was making than it did with me. We didn't say much for the next hour but later, when we'd both showered and changed back into street clothes, she surprised me with an invitation to join her in the pool room for one of her cranberry juice cocktails.

"You're in good shape for your...uh... size," she said as we sat down.

I laughed. "You mean, for the extra flab I seem to be carrying nowadays."

She grinned. "You are carrying a couple of extra pounds, but that isn't what I meant. Really. You aren't much bigger than Sarah Leah but you're a lot stronger. She can't do the treadmill at the speed you were doing, that's for sure."

I shrugged, not telling her the treadmill was my best output.

"I've been meaning to call you," she said. "I behaved like an idiot the other day and I owe you an apology. At the time I was hating myself for being glad Caro was dead, and sorry for her at the same time and... My sister... Anyway, I had no business taking it out on you."

"Forget it," I said amiably. "You had good reason."

"Thanks." We were quiet for a while, sipping our drinks, then she asked, "How's the investigation going? Do you know who, uh, who killed her?"

I shook my head. "I know who didn't, and that's something. I don't know what the police know, but I don't think they're any closer to finding the killer than I am."

"So what do you do now?"

"Ask more questions."

"Of whom?" Her tone turned sharp.

"Anyone who will listen. She was out somewhere Saturday night, and she was with someone. That someone may have been the one who killed her, or he may not be. He might know something that would help, another person may have seen them, or know something. At the moment there's no way of telling what might be important, what could lead to her killer. I'm sure Lieutenant Morgan has a dozen men out asking all kinds of questions." A dozen men was a big exaggeration but I had a feeling she might be more willing to talk to me if she thought she was going to be talking to Sam next. "Which reminds me, I've got a few questions for your ex-brother-in-law. Didn't you say he was working in a used car agency?"

She gave me a sour glance. "Do you think he killed Caro?"

"No. I mean, I don't know. I suppose he could have. I've not thought about him before."

"Well, don't bother. He's a wimp." She stopped, thought a moment. "On the other hand he might know who she was out with. It would be like him to be following her around like a whipped puppy."

The contempt in her voice raised my eyebrows. I thought she was fond of him. Or had been, anyway. She had certainly sounded that way when I'd talked to her before.

"I guess I thought it was all over between them when Caro married," I said.

She gave a harsh laugh. "It was. Actually, I don't think there ever was anything between them anyway, except for her using him and him being a fool." Her face twisted into a bitter grimace. "One thing none of her men seemed to realize was that Caro was a cold, calculating woman. I doubt very much that she ever had an affair with anyone. She was too careful, too cautious. Caro always had her eye on the main chance and Don wasn't it."

"Then why did—"

"Why did my sister take a kitchen stepladder, climb up on the railing, and jump off the Narrows Bridge?" Her eyes filled with tears. She brushed them away angrily. "Because she loved him, I guess. I begged her to cool it, to just let things ride, that Caro would dump him eventually, but no, she had to have it out with him, and the result was he walked out on her. And she walked out on life."

"Sara, I'm sorry. I shouldn't have brought it up. I'd like to talk to Don but I could have asked someone else."

"No, not your fault, I started it myself. I

can't seem to get over... Look, I really do want her killer caught, to have it all over with. Maybe then I can have some peace. As it is now I'm pulled first one way and then another.''

I started to say something sympathetic but she went on: ''And don't tell me I need to see a shrink. I'm already seeing one. Don is working at that big pricey used car place in the University district. I don't remember the street but it's just north of the Meany Hotel. It's the one that has that antique Stutz Bearcat on a turntable in the front corner window. Lean on him a little. Isn't that what they say in the movies? He's such a spineless jerk you won't have to lean very hard.'' She got up, gave me a damp smile, and walked away.

Between grief and hate Sara was tearing herself apart. I hoped her psychologist could help her but I had a feeling nothing would help until Caro's killer was caught and she could start to forget.

TWENTY-SIX

SHERRY CAME RUNNING INTO the pool room just as I was preparing to leave. As gorgeous as ever despite her harried expression, she said, "Oh, Demary, I'm so sorry. That awful Scott had me standing under the lights for an hour shooting close-ups he should have done in Reykjavik. I hate working with the lights. They show up every stupid flaw you've got." She collapsed into the chair across from me and called to the waitress to please bring her a diet cola.

Blessing my luck—I'd been hard-pressed to think of a way I could bring Scott into a conversation without rousing her curiosity—I expressed my sympathy and gave her time to catch her breath.

"You don't sound as if you're too fond of him," I said finally. "I thought he was your favorite photographer."

"Oh, he is. I'm just tired. No one is a better photographer. He's a genius with a lens, but he's a pain to work with, especially when we're out of the country. He says we can't come back for a second take so the light has to be exactly right, the background has to be just so, and then when Jocko, his assistant, has everything set, half the time Scott's gone off, drinking wine in a bistro with one of his local pals, or taking pictures of a broken-down wall. We lose a whole day sometimes."

"Oh?" I gave her my best impression of great surprise. "I would have thought you all stuck together like glue until the job was done. Those overseas jaunts must cost the magazines a mint."

"Actually, they do. And some of the smaller mags won't use Scott for that very reason. A lot of girls won't work with him either, for the same reason. They don't like spending a week on what should be a three-day shoot. But he is s-o-o good."

"Gee. I wish someone would pay me for an extra week in Paris."

"To do what? Wander around all by yourself? When you've been through the Louvre fifteen times already? It's not that much fun, Demary. And you can't just take off and tour the countryside. If he shows back up you have to be there. It's all right for him to be late, or not show—he runs the shoot—but brother, the rest of us better be standing by.''

''I thought the models were the important ones.''

''We can throw our weight around some but believe me, it's the guy with the camera who runs the show. For one thing, he can make you look great in the worst outfit ever put together, or he can make you look like a potato sack tied in the middle.''

Sherry was practically writing my script for me. ''What do you mean, you're all by yourself? Where does Scott get all his local pals?''

''Beats me. Most of them don't look like the type I'd care to pal around with, that's for sure.''

''Oh? What kind of people? Men? Women? Old? Young?''

She shrugged. ''Mostly older guys that look kind of, oh, I don't know, like…I guess they just don't look like the kind I want to know. One thing I will say for Scott though, he doesn't bring them around the shoot. I've only seen him with locals by chance. Mostly when I've been ticked off at standing around a half a day and gone looking for him.''

''Well, at least you've got the other people you work with to run around with.''

''Everybody else is the same as me. They've seen Paris. We're on a job and we'd like to get it done and go home. I know it sounds glamorous to be going to Corinth, or some other name place, but half the time it's hot, and dirty, your feet hurt, and there isn't any decent shower. Or it's so cold your feet are frozen and there isn't any shower at all. To tell the truth, Demary, if I wasn't getting close to being over the hill I wouldn't work with Scott anymore either.'' She traced the line of her chin with her fingers. ''The new girls coming up are still in their teens. As fresh as spring flowers. I'm the same age you are, and without a photographer as good as Scott I'd be all through.''

I scowled at her. I don't consider thirty-something old. She is so lovely to look at I thought she must be suffering from some kind of depression, but she wasn't, and when I looked at her again, blanking my mind to the

fact that she looked perfect to me, I saw she
was right. She was beginning to show her age.

She laughed, her eyes crinkling with amuse-
ment. "Good grief, Demary, get that expression off your face. I'm not about to start choos-
ing a gravesite or anything. I'm just getting too
old for the cosmetics ads. I'm still okay with
the big couture houses. I've never had to watch
my figure and that old gal way back at that
charm school Mother sent me to really knew
how to teach the runway strut. I may not be
number one anymore, but my agent doesn't
have any problem booking me shows. Anyway,
I don't much care. I'm getting close to my goal
and as soon as I make it I'm gone."

Sherry had been working toward the horse
ranch she wants for as long as I can remember.
I think she started saving five minutes after she
had her first ride in the pony ring at Woodland
Park.

"Well, at least you don't always go to Paris.
He must stay on the job better when you go
other places," I said.

"Don't I wish. Although Paris is the worst.
But the last time we were in Germany, in Cologne, he was terrible. He must have changed

locations a dozen times. First the light would be wrong, too much shadow, then the background was killing the clothes, or not enough contrast, then something else. I swear, it took us forever to get the right shots."

"When was this?"

"Last spring. Funny, now that I think about it, twice when he didn't show up on time I saw him talking to an old fellow from an antique shop. I mean, not having a beer or anything, just talking."

"Oh? How do you know he was from an antique shop?"

"I'd seen him the time before when we were in Cologne. And actually the place was more of a junk shop than a real antique gallery. I was wandering around the cathedral square when I saw Scott on one of the side streets. He was going in the general direction of our hotel so I followed him, meaning to catch up and go on to the hotel with him. Instead he went into this seedy-looking little antique place. He was at the back of the shop talking to this man when I looked in the window, so I just went on by."

"Maybe he was dickering to buy something.

Maybe for his grandparents. They seem to have some nice things around.''

"I don't think so. The shop was too grubby.''

"What was it called?'' I asked idly.

She eyed me uncertainly. "Why are you so interested in Scott all of a sudden?''

It was time to back off. Quickly. "You're the one who brought him up, not me. I'm just making conversation. And it's time I quit.'' I looked at my watch. "Good grief, I'll say it is. I'll leave you to your workout, kid. I did my stint with Sara Lee.''

With that I got up, blew her a kiss, and headed for the door. Leaving, I was much afraid, a bewildered Sherry staring after me. She had told me that morning she was taking a couple of weeks off. She was going to take her mother to Albuquerque to visit relatives. So she was safe for now, but before she was scheduled for her next job out of the country I'd either have to have enough on Scott to turn him over to the Feds or warn her away from him. And that wouldn't be easy. Sherry was nothing if not loyal to her friends, and despite her grousing I know she considered Scott a friend.

I didn't think the man was dangerous; he had no record of violence of any kind. In fact, he didn't really have any kind of record. But you never know. With the amount of money I was guessing was at stake, he might be more dangerous than I thought. After all, if I was right, he'd been fencing counterfeit for a lot of years. And if he and his grandfather were behind the La Tour scam... Well, I didn't think it was a good idea for Sherry to be off in the middle of Europe with him.

TWENTY-SEVEN

I WISHED I'D THOUGHT to ask Sara Lee how to identify Don Ward. As it was I'd have to go in cold. Considering what my car looked like, however, I thought I'd be convincing as a prospective buyer. The Toyota appeared to be on its last gasp, but actually it was in perfect running condition despite its age and its many dents and dings. Some time ago I'd done a big favor for a local garage owner, a very big favor—I'd kept his daughter out of jail—and his way of saying thanks was to keep the working parts of my car in "like new" shape.

As it happened I didn't need to look for Don, nor plan an approach. When I pulled into the lot in front of the big window housing the Stutz Bearcat on its turntable the first person I saw was Joey zipping around the place on his skateboard.

He swished up beside my window before I had the motor turned off.

"Joey, what are you doing in the U district on that thing?" I demanded. "You'll get yourself killed in the traffic around here."

He gave me one of his Joey looks that said I not only had no clue to life in general, I was six yards behind him when it came to detecting.

"Your man's inside. The one in the blue Izod shirt," he said, nodding toward the showroom. "Looks like a nerd to me but he's the one in the alley. Used a different car every night. Trying to impress her. Strictly a loser. Rubber backbone."

I gawked at him. "Where in the— Where did you get that information?"

"Don't worry about it," he said, smug. "It's the straight skinny. I couldn't find out for sure where they met but he always headed north so it was probably over around Lake City somewhere."

"How..."

"Shoving off," he said, and promptly did so, sailing across the lot and down the sidewalk at a clip that took him out of earshot before the Izod shirt was halfway out the showroom door.

Don, if that's who it was, kept coming. I stepped out of the Toyota to face him, making up my mind as I did on what tactic to use. Both Sara and Joey had him pegged as a weak character so a blunt approach should work.

"Is that your brat...I mean, boy?" he asked, altering his tone in mid-sentence as the idea hit his mind that I might be a customer. I could practically hear him change gears.

"I thought maybe he was yours the way he took off out of here when he saw you coming," I said blandly.

"Oh," he said, momentarily nonplussed.

"Are you Don Ward?" I asked.

It took him a couple of breaths to recover. "Yes. Yes, I am," he said finally, a professional smile struggling to his face. "What can I show you?" He gave the Toyota a quick once-over, undoubtedly assessing its trade-in value.

"You can tell me about your relationship with Caro Gray," I said coolly.

For a second it looked like I'd made a mistake, that he was going to turn around and walk off. I could see the thought in his eyes, but he did answer. "It was over a long time ago," he said in a tight voice. "What business is it of yours anyway? Who are you? You're not a cop or you'd be flashing a badge."

"Never mind what I am," I said sharply, feeling like a character in a B movie. I wanted to keep him thinking I was official if possible. "Let's talk about you and your role in Caro Gray's death."

"No," he whispered, his face suddenly going chalk white. "I mean, I don't have any role. I don't know anything about—"

"Come on, Ward, let's not waste time." I interrupted him in what I hoped was an authoritative tone. "You were seen, not once, a dozen times or more, bringing her home through the alley. Now let's—"

With a gasping, moaning sound that was part denial, part agony, and a whole lot of fear, Don Ward went down on his knees, tipped over sideways, and lay there on the blacktop wailing like a two-year-old.

I'd envisioned him doing a number of things—such as telling me to get lost—but falling apart wasn't one of them. He wasn't stupid—he'd managed to get a college degree— and he sure wasn't puny, in fact, he was a big husky guy. What in the world was the matter with him? I stood there gaping at him like an idiot for at least a full minute before I pulled myself together and nudged him with the toe of my Reebok.

"Get up off there," I said astringently. "And put a sock in it. You sound like a demented alley cat."

Joey whirled around the hood of my car and jumped off his board to look at Ward. "What's the matter with him? Having some kind of a fit?" he asked.

I jerked my thumb toward the sidewalk. "Get out of here," I hissed.

He made a face at me but zipped off obediently.

Ward didn't seem to have noticed him but he stopped his blubbering.

I nudged him with my toe again. "Get up."

In a moment he pushed himself into a sitting position and leaned against the front wheel of the Toyota. "Go away, leave me alone," he muttered.

"Fat chance!" I could see Joey keeping an eye on things from two cars over. "Come on, let's hear it."

Ward let his breath out with a weary sigh. "I didn't kill her. I hadn't seen her for nearly a week." Tears ran down his cheeks and dripped off the end of his chin. "She said she wouldn't meet me again, and if I came to the house she'd tell Steven I was harassing her." He gulped back a sob. "Harassing her! As if I would! She knew how much I loved her."

"So you killed her." I knew when I said it that he hadn't done any such thing.

"No!" He straightened up and got to his feet. "No, I didn't kill her. And furthermore—" He laughed, a harsh sound with no humor in it. "And furthermore, I have a really excellent alibi. I was in Northgate Hospital. From seven Saturday night and until after noon on Sunday. I and six other members of the firm. We were all very sick. In fact the doctor didn't release one of the women until Tuesday. Food poisoning from a catered buffet dinner served right here." He nodded at the showroom behind us, showing the first sign of animation I'd seen. I had a feeling some poor food emporium was about to face a horrendous lawsuit.

I looked at him thoughtfully. "My name is Demary Jones, and I'm not from the police,"

I said in a less hostile but certainly not conciliatory tone. The jerk should have come forward
long ago. "Have you talked to the police?"

"No. Why should I?"

"Because she was murdered, and in a particularly brutal way I might add, and you were
having an affair with her."

"Having an affair?" His voice rose into the
soprano range before he could get it back under
control. "Whoever you are, you don't know
what you're talking about and you certainly
never knew Caro. Caro wouldn't...I loved her.
I loved her from the first minute I saw her. I
wanted to marry her but she wouldn't hear of
my divorcing Kathy. She didn't believe in divorce."

She sure didn't.

"And by the time Kathy jumped off the
bridge Caro was already married to Steven. Is
that it?" I asked.

"Yes, and you can believe it or not." His
shoulders sagged. "I'm sorry Kathy was so
foolish but it just doesn't matter anymore."

I honestly didn't know whether to feel some
sympathy for the guy or give him a good swift
kick in the behind. He was pathetic.

"So why were you sneaking around with her whenever Steven went out of town?" I asked.

"We weren't sneaking," he snapped with a mild spurt of temper.

"No? What were you doing then? And why bring her home through the alley if your visits were so innocent?"

"She got lonesome with Steven gone so much. She let me take her out to dinner, sometimes to a show. That was all. I brought her home through the alley so her snoopy neighbors wouldn't notice she was out and go running to Steven with a bunch of lies."

I almost believed him. Almost. Shows how gullible I can be sometimes.

TWENTY-EIGHT

JOEY OPENED the back door and slid his skateboard in before getting in beside me.

"Not the right guy, huh?" he said. He stared out the window, frowning. "Have to be one cool cat, pretty cold-blooded, to cut a lady's throat. Didn't see him that way myself. Crybaby type."

"Do you want me to take you home?" I asked. I didn't want to discuss Ward.

"No." He parodied a grin, showing his braces. "Nope, you can let me off at your place. I'm supposed to be at my orthodontist's over on Stoneway five minutes ago."

"I'll take you." I glanced at him, trying to smile in return. "I make better time than a skateboard."

We didn't say anything else. He got out with a brief good-bye. Don Ward's behavior had depressed both of us. Plus, he was the last viable suspect I had.

MARTHA HAD LEFT a note—she'd gone out to lunch—saying she'd be back by one-thirty. Which suited me fine. I locked myself in my office, turned on my computer, typed in the report of my "talk" with Don Ward, and then sat staring at the ceiling, trying to think.

I went back over everyday, mentally dredging up everything I'd seen or heard, hoping something would click. Nothing did. I was out of suspects, unless I wanted to count Daniel, and I was no nearer a motive than I'd been a week ago when I'd first heard of Caro's death. All the obvious suspects had solid alibis and I didn't know of anyone else who was even close to her, let alone had a motive.

"Maybe it was a wandering maniac," I muttered.

But if that was the case, who was the man young Jenny had seen bring Caro home that night? If he'd had nothing to do with her death why hadn't he contacted Sam's office? The story had been in the paper and on TV several times asking for help and/or information.

Who was he? He was out there, somewhere, and somewhere in my notes there must be a clue to his identity.

I turned to the computer again and, on impulse, hit the print button. I was surprised when my big HP LaserJet spewed out sixty-two single-spaced pages. Looking at my notes on the screen I hadn't realized I'd keyboarded in anywhere near that much. Before I'd read more than a couple of pages, however, I realized I'd made a stupid mistake. When I'd transferred my original file on Caro to the data base, I'd somehow combined Caro's and the Hon. Violet's, and the data base automatically picked up and correlated the two. My data base program had been designed for me by a computer whiz kid I knew. It contained several features not in the commercial databases, one of which was an automatic star symbol beside any fact or name that was within the file in another context.

The printout was literally strewn with stars. Part of them were due to the fact that both women lived in the same neighborhood, but some didn't make any sense and I wondered if the program had developed a glitch.

I record any conversation I have as close to

word for word as I can, adding my conclusions or observations at the end. The system has always worked well for me but, of course, combining two unrelated cases had scrambled the whole thing and it was going to take me hours of work to get it in order.

Mentally kicking myself for being so stupid, I clicked on the cut and paste icon and started separating. At least looking at every conversation again might clarify my mind regarding Caro's case; I was pretty sure I already had Violet's taken care of. All I needed was some hard proof to convince her, and I was reasonably sure that would be forthcoming from the German authorities.

A while later Martha came in, sympathized, and offered to help sort but I told her no. I was beginning to see a pattern that I hadn't even suspected and I needed to work on it by myself. Something Joey had said earlier had nagged at me; my mind had made a quantum leap to set me on another track. He'd said that Caro's killer had to be one cool cat and pretty cold-blooded too, a factor I hadn't considered before. I did now.

I made several phone calls, confirming some

conclusions, eliminating others. Around four, when I was through sorting, I called Sherry and asked her to describe Scott.

Puzzled, she did so, then asked, "What in the world do you think he's done, Demary? I saw him this afternoon, just a little while ago, and asked him if he knew you but he said he'd never even heard your name before."

My hand turned slippery on the receiver. "Sherry, what did you say to him? Did you tell him I'd been asking you about him?"

"Well, yes, I did. But what—"

"Sherry, listen to me, I think the man is dangerous. Are your parents home?" I knew they didn't live far from her apartment.

"What...? Oh, yes, Mom called a few minutes ago. What are you talking about, Demary? Scott is about the least dangerous person I know."

"Trust me on this, Sherry. Call your dad and ask him to come get you, and stay in your apartment with the door locked until he gets there. And don't let anyone else in. No one, and especially not Scott. I don't think he realizes you know as much as you do but there is no sense taking any chances."

"What in the world...I don't know anything."

"Sherry, listen to me. I think Scott is laundering counterfeit twenty-dollar bills all over Europe and you are probably the only one who can prove it. Now will you do what I say?"

She didn't answer for a moment, but finally agreed to call her father, albeit reluctantly. We'd known each other for a long time and she knew I wasn't one to cry wolf.

I hesitated after I'd hung up, thinking maybe I ought to call the police too, but decided it wasn't necessary. Scott couldn't have any idea of what I knew, nor would he realize right off how much Sherry had seen, so if she got out of the apartment she'd be all right until I could get the facts lined up, and get them to the right people. This was one case where I had no intention of rushing in on my own.

My next call, on a different tack, was to Daniel's office. It was too early for him to have gone home. He wasn't in, but when I told the woman who answered that my call was urgent she agreed to see if she could get in touch with him and have him get back to me. Government agencies seem to have a built-in reluctance to giving out any kind of information, and certainly not cell-phone numbers. I gave her both my office and home number in case Daniel didn't have them handy. I wanted to talk to him before I did anything else. He deserved that much, at least.

Sam was next, and he wasn't in either but he was due back any minute. I left a message for him, then called to Martha to come in.

She listened, her smooth, chocolate-colored face totally blank as I told her what I thought had happened. "Get it down on paper and I'll fax a copy to Sam's office, then I think it would be a good idea if we both got out of here," she said, sounding serious.

I laughed. "Let's not get carried away. If I'm right, he did murder Caro, but I doubt very much that he'd ever believe I could figure it out."

"Don't be silly, Demary. He's not stupid and he knows where you are."

"All right, go lock up and put the closed sign in the window. I'll do a brief précis for you to fax, send the whole lot e-mail, and we'll go home."

"No, don't go home, Demary. He knows where you live too."

"Well, I've got to go somewhere," I said, humoring her. "Where would you suggest?"

"Sam's house."

"Wha-a-t? What are you suggesting, you naughty girl," I said, kidding her. My fingers were busy automatically typing in what I knew or had deduced.

"I mean it, Demary. That's the last place he'll look. You can park around the back and stay in the car until he gets home."

I hit the print button. She was so worried she was beginning to scare me. "Oh, all right. I'll take my cell phone and go somewhere until Sam calls."

She took the printout and went out to the fax. The machine made a little buzzing noise. I heard music playing somewhere in the distance. A country-western tune.

We left together five minutes later.

TWENTY-NINE

FEELING ROTTEN, I stopped at the QFC on my way home and bought myself some comfort food. I was sure I was right about who had killed Caro, and it wouldn't be hard to prove, but I didn't feel good about any part of it. Several innocent people were going to be hurt. A trial and its aftermath left a messy trail behind.

I pulled into my driveway, glad that Joey wasn't sitting on my porch steps as he frequently was. I needed a few minutes alone to think before I called Sam to let him know where I'd be.

Some hard-boiled PI you are, I thought derisively as I unlocked the front door. I gave it a shove and bent down to pick up the flyer someone had left on the mat.

A millisecond later a huge roar of sound thundered in my ears and the door flew off its hinges. It sailed through the air just above my head like a big square Frisbee, smashing through the porch railings as if they were made of tissue paper. The blast tossed me off the porch and into the rhododendron beside the steps. Chunks of what I later learned was plaster and wood hit my back.

My head met the ground with an audible thud. I heard it. Scraps of my hall carpet swirled through the air. There was a tinkling sound as shards of glass fell on top of the Toyota.

I had time to be glad again that Joey hadn't been waiting for me, and then everything was gone.

I WOKE UP in a hard, narrow bed. The hands of a big round clock on the wall opposite me pointed to six-twenty-five. Being the sharp detective that I am, I immediately deduced I was in the hospital again; it was evening—twilight filled what sky I could see in the window—and I wasn't suffering from anything serious. I had a rotten headache but I could move everything, cautiously, and there was no one standing over me with a worried look on their face. In fact, I was the only one in the room. I couldn't think why I was there but I didn't seem to be hurt much so I went back to sleep.

WHEN I WOKE UP again the situation was somewhat different. It was still late evening but there were a number of people around, and I woke with a shriek that startled the nurse beside me into dropping the bottle she was about to hang on the drip stand beside the bed.

"My house!" I wailed. "My beautiful house. What happened to my house?" I sat up with a jerk that nearly tore a strip off the top of my head.

"It's all right, it's all right," Martha's soft buttery voice came from my left somewhere. (Everything was a bit fuzzy.) "It's all right, Demary, it can be fixed. Lay back down, you have a mild concussion."

Struggling to get out of bed, unsuccessfully, I was suddenly violently ill.

"That will be enough of that," the nurse said sharply. "You calm down now or I'll have to give you a shot."

"You sod off!" Martha again, apparently speaking to the nurse, and *not* sounding buttery.

"If you're going to make a habit of this

maybe we ought to reserve you a regular room." Sam's voice. The fuzz cleared and I saw him now, standing at the foot of the bed. The hands on the clock behind him pointed to six-forty-five. I'd either lost twenty-four hours or less than twenty minutes had passed since I had looked at the clock.

Martha squeezed my hand. "The house can be fixed, Demary, so don't get your knickers in a twist. You got bashed around a bit, that's all."

I smiled weakly. Trust Martha to get my priorities straight.

I started to ask the same banal old question, what happened?, but before I could get the words out my own GP, Dr. Mack, came striding in.

He took my pulse, shined a light into my eyes, and nodded at Sam. "She'll be okay. Bad bump on the head but the pictures don't show anything serious."

"How about telling me?" I snapped. I hate it when a doctor talks to someone else about me when I'm right there, acting as if I'm either unconscious or moronic.

"See, told you so," Dr. Mack said equitably,

still looking at Sam. "She's perfectly normal." He smiled down at me. "You are all right, Demary, just bruised a bit, but I'm going to keep you here overnight for observation, and tomorrow morning an MRI. This is the third whack on the head you've taken in less than a year and I want to be sure you don't have any residual damage, so don't argue." He patted my shoulder, nodded at the nurse, and went out before I could say anything. Not that I had any intention of arguing. Tomorrow would be soon enough.

WHEN I WOKE UP the next time I saw Sam asleep in a recliner chair by the window. The clock registered three-twenty-five. It was black outside.

I was very touched. I didn't think I'd made a sound but he opened his eyes and smiled at me. "How do you feel?" he asked, getting up and coming over to give me a gentle kiss. "Headache gone?"

"Mostly. What happened, Sam?"

"He planted a load of gelignite in the hall and wired it to the doorknob. How you're still alive I don't know. When you were thrown off the porch it put you below the worst of it, but the blast took off most of the front of the house and broke windows in your neighbors' houses on both sides. No one else was hurt.''

Tears trickled down the sides of my face.

"If you're crying about your confounded house I'm going to leave," he said, wiping my tears away with the palm of his hand. "The fire department has already sealed the front, so don't worry about it. It can be fixed.''

"No, I'm not...I just want...''

"I know, you want to know what happened." He gave me another gentle kiss. "That's why I came back.''

"How did he get in my house? What happened to my security system? And where did he get the gelignite?'' I just couldn't bear the thought that he'd been inside, prowling through my things.

"The bomb squad is working on all those little questions but they don't know yet.''

"Did you catch him?''

He smiled. "Yes, Demary, we caught him. He was at SeaTac, cameras draped over his shoulder, and a ticket to Zurich in his hand. He was on our list, we knew Caro knew him, but we didn't have anything to tie him to her murder. A shoulder bag with a false bottom packed with bogus twenty-dollar bills will keep him in a cell until we sort it out.''

I went home the next day, or rather, to my parents' house for some TLC, and later to the extra bedroom in Sherry's apartment. I was stiff and sore but, as Martha said, I'd simply got bashed around a bit.

It was over a week before the several agencies involved had it "sorted out" enough to charge Scott Meyer with Caro's murder, in addition to everything else he could be charged with. The evidence was there, as I knew it would be, when I finally remembered Sherry's remark about Scott knowing Caro, thinking her gorgeous despite all the beautiful women he photographed. That and Joey's remark about a cool cat made me realize it was never a crime of passion. It was the same old number-one motive, money, the bottom line. And it had nothing to do with Uncle George's millions, which in the end he had left entirely to the city of Alameda. Scott Meyer killed Caro because her scheme to get even with the Honorable Violet Barcasie for snubbing her was threatening to end the counterfeit enterprise he and his grandfather had been operating for twenty years. A enterprise she didn't know a thing about.

I would guess it started when Caro tried to ingratiate herself with the Hon. Violet. By that time, however, she had already made herself disliked by most of the neighborhood and Violet rejected her advances with contempt, and probably with considerable arrogance.

Furious, and knowing both Scott and his grandparents—she had met them when she first arrived in Seattle and lived in a poky little apartment near the Parricks' place—and knowing Mr. Parrick's considerable artistic talent, she persuaded him to paint the fake La Tour as a "joke."

When Scott discovered what she and his grandfather had done, he tried to talk Caro into passing it off as the real thing, to be satisfied with the million dollars Violet was willing to pay for it. He misjudged Violet to start with; he hadn't expected her to have it authenticated so thoroughly, and he certainly misjudged Caro. She had no intention of not letting Violet know she'd been had. When she refused to lis-

ten to him, he made up his mind to kill her and
in a totally cold-blooded way he set out to implicate as many other people as possible.

He called her Saturday and said he needed
to talk to her. She was nearly over her cold by
then and probably didn't care about how Scott
saw her anyway, so she agreed to meet him for
dinner. They had several drinks before they ate,
or Caro did—she wasn't the teetotaler she pretended to be—a bottle of wine with their meal,
which Caro drank alone, and several after-
dinner drinks. Again, Caro had several, Scott
had one. The waitress where they dined took
note of what he drank because she thought they
had come together, and was nervous about
serving him too much, naturally supposing him
to be driving. Washington State has very tough
laws regarding the server's liability. They left
together in Caro's car with Scott driving. By
that time, between the liquor and the antihistamines she had taken, she was close to passing
out. He brought her home—parking in the drive
because Caro kept the electronic opener under
the seat and he couldn't find it—and walked
her into the backyard. She was apparently so
far gone by that time he didn't have any trouble

pouring, or forcing, a pint of gin down her throat.

He did choose Daniel's garage deliberately. Caro had told him about Daniel when she first met him and his grandfather. He had never even seen Daniel himself but he knew enough about Caro's plane "death" to know leaving her in his garage would cloud the investigation. He'd poured the gin into her for the same reason. Anything to confuse the crime team.

He knew any inquiry into his own relationship with her would put the counterfeiting business in jeopardy and it was far too profitable to allow that to happen. And certainly not on the whim of a woman he didn't like. He, of all the men I knew of, had Caro pegged from the very beginning.

One thing I was thankful for was I hadn't put Sherry in harm's way as I'd feared. He must have gone straight to my house after talking to Sherry, and may even have called the airline from there because he booked his ticket to Zurich within a few minutes of my talking to her. He no doubt has a fat bank account there somewhere.

Again, his motive for destroying my house,

and me in the bargain if possible, was simply to confuse the investigation. It wasn't desperation—he had no idea how much I'd unraveled—it was a simple cold-blooded operation to protect his source of income. If I'd been dead and Scott in Europe somewhere taking pictures of broken-down walls, Sam would have had an impossible time tying it all together. Or at least so Scott must have thought. He wasn't to know I had it all on my computer, or that Martha knew everything I knew, or that we had faxed it all to Sam.

I didn't have to give evidence, nor did I attend his trial. I did hear all about it, but despite the reams of testimony, the sometimes pathetic, sometimes deplorable, stories that were told about Caro, I never have been able to make up my mind about her.

Was she schizophrenic, or just a lost butterfly who couldn't find her place in life? Was Steven right? Did she get a divorce in Mexico or was Daniel right and she had amnesia? Or was Martha right, that she was narcissistic to the point she never gave a thought to anyone except herself?

Whatever was true, she didn't deserve to die the way she did.

MURDER, MAYHEM
And
MISTLETOE

Terence Faherty, Aileen Schumacher, Wendi Lee, Bill Crider

Four new tales of Christmas crimes from four of today's most popular mystery writers.

THE HEADLESS MAGI

What do several alarming calls to a crisis center and vandalism at a local nativity scene have in common? Owen Keane, metaphysical sleuth in Terence Faherty's Edgar-nominated series is about to find out!

CHRISTMAS CACHE

Aileen Schumacher's New Mexico sleuth, Tory Travers, finds herself undertaking a challenging Christmas puzzle: an international network of art thieves, a backyard full of cash, and a mysterious shooting.

STOCKING STUFFER

Wendi Lee's Boston P.I. Angela Matelli uncovers a case of shoplifting that leads to murder...

THE EMPTY MANGER

Bill Crider's easygoing Texas sheriff Dan Rhodes has his hands full with a "living" manger scene in downtown Clearview, especially when the body of the local councilwoman is found dead behind it.

Available November 2001
at your favorite retail outlet.

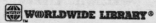

WORLDWIDE LIBRARY®

WMMM

DEAD MEN DIE

A DEMARY JONES MYSTERY

When Demary Jones stumbles over a man's naked corpse on the front steps of her temporary digs, it gives new meaning to the phrase "dead man's walk." Suspicious questions from the investigating detective rattle her almost as much as the nagging fear that she'd interrupted the dumping of the body, and that the killer would be back to clean up any loose ends—like her.

The picture darkens when ten thousand dollars in counterfeit money is wired to Demary's bank account and the treasury department is ready to foreclose on her freedom. Though jail might be the safest place for her right now, she's racing to expose the sinister truth before a killer can hide all his secrets in blood.

E. L. LARKIN

Available December 2001 at your favorite retail outlet.

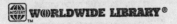
WORLDWIDE LIBRARY®

WELL406

CRIMES OF

Passion

Sometimes Cupid's aim can be deadly.

This Valentine's Day, Worldwide Mystery brings you
four stories of passionate betrayal and deadly crime
in one gripping anthology.

Crimes of Passion features FIRE AND ICE,
NIGHT FLAMES, ST. VALENTINE'S DIAMOND,
and THE LOVEBIRDS by favorite romance authors
Maggie Price and B.J. Daniels,
and top mystery authors Nancy Means Wright
and Jonathan Harrington.

Where red isn't just for roses.

Available January 2002 at your favorite retail outlet.

WORLDWIDE LIBRARY®

WCOP

KILLER
A Charlie Greene Mystery
COMMUTE

California literary agent Charlie Greene starts her weeklong vacation by shutting off the phone, putting out the cat—and finding the body of her neighbor slumped in his SUV. With nothing but her track record for stumbling onto bodies to incriminate her, Charlie becomes the prime suspect.

It seems as if Charlie's dearly departed neighbor had some dangerous secrets involving bundles of hidden cash. Soon a strategically placed bomb, a temporary loss of hearing, a stint in jail—all topped off by the stunning events unfolding in her own backyard—lead Charlie to the inescapable conclusion that vacations really are murder.

"...clever and original plotting..."
—*Publishers Weekly*

MARLYS MILLHISER

Available December 2001 at your favorite retail outlet.

WORLDWIDE LIBRARY®

WMM405